Unshakable

Casts of Silver Series:
Book 4

K.J. ROWE

Ark House Press
arkhousepress.com

Cataloguing in Publication Data:
Title: Unshakable
ISBN: 978-1-7636468-7-2 (pbk)
Subjects: Fiction
Other Authors/Contributors: Rowe, K.J.

Design by initiateagency.com

"And we know that in all things God works for the good of those who love him, who have been called according to his purpose."
Romans 8:28 (NIV)

For my good friend, the late Senior Sergeant Tony, who always said I should have been a policewoman. God had other plans for me too.

CHAPTER ONE

ick Marshall bolted upright. Wrestling off the covers, he swung his legs to the floor and held his head in his hands. Breathing in through his nose... and out through his mouth, he tried to calm his racing heart.

That dream. It was tormenting him. Replaying the night of his inaugural first-responder call. He was told that the memory would fade, but it was still as vivid as when it happened, and he couldn't move past it.

With shaky legs Nick rose from his bed and moved to his dresser. His hands gripped the sides of the distressed oak and he raised his eyes to the mirror. His complexion was ashen in the blue moonlight. Wide, unblinking eyes stared back, distorting his features so that Nick couldn't bear to look for too long.

He lowered his head and closed his eyes. Desperate to work out why it haunted him, he allowed the dream to play over again.

The evening had been clear. Quiet. Still.

Stars littered the indigo sky above the silhouetted, suburban countryside while a quarter moon hung low in the sky. He tilted his head back and took in a long deep breath of the intoxicating scent of jasmine.

Without warning, the peaceful landscape shattered. Sharp flashes of red and blue speared the atmosphere around him, and he squinted against the cool lights.

Distant sirens drew near while frantic voices cried out and he whirled around, eyes searching. With a strong voice he had called out, "Where are you?"

First responders, forensic crash units and ambulance vehicles appeared around him. Tires screeched as they slid over a shimmering blackened substance covering the road.

Blood.

An earthy scent with a metallic undernote tingled in his nose as it permeated his sinuses. Panic gripped him while he watched it pool around his boots, cementing him to where he stood.

Another strangled cry rang out from the shadows and Nick strained to see where the victim was. The cars nearby looked like rumpled beds after a bad night's sleep and dread weighed in his gut at what he was trying to see.

Then he saw it.

Two, young men. What was left of one, and the other with features undisguisable, mouth agape as he shrieked and gasped. His clothing shredded by the harsh surface of the bitumen, revealed flesh torn from his bones and a number of dislocations. His foot was twisted back behind him and a hand lay detached not far from him.

Cars crawled past at glacial pace, drivers and passengers watched with emotionless faces as the young man cried out for his mum, while his wild and terrified eyes seemed to almost pop from his whitened face.

Nick looked to the left, to the right, trying to block out the man's screams. Where was everyone? Why was no one helping him?

He cried out again; the sound was garbled as if he was under water...

Nick drew in a shaky breath and pushed off from his dresser; restless. Pulling his damp T-shirt off his chest, he paced around his room.

Why did the dream always end there?

Why did he dream that no one was around, when in reality the roadside had crawled with aid workers? And why couldn't he move – why was he stuck to the spot?

What was it about that night that his brain wouldn't let go of?

Was it just the two young people who were out having what they thought was fun in their hotted-up cars and their lives were cut short?

Was it seeing a body smeared over the road?

Was it watching a life slip away from a person? Or was it something deeper?

Nick ran his hands over his head and groaned. Returning to his bed, he lay on his back and focused on breathing.

"Dear God," Nicks voice was hushed as he spoke into the silence. "Help me move past this. I have a job to do, and this feels like a shadow in my mind that won't go away, no matter how much counseling I have. Am I broken? Or are you trying to speak to me?"

That accident had been almost ten months ago, but it was still as vivid in his dreams as if he and Geoff had just pulled up in responding to the call-out.

His mind turned to that night. His friend, Trent Vaughan, had called in not long after he'd got home from the accident site. The house had been empty, with his sisters, Beth and Lauren, away at university and his parents out for dinner. Nick had arrived home, entered the living room, and just stared at the wall. He shuddered at the memory; he'd never zoned out like that before. The counselor had since said it was a form of anxiety attack. Anxiety attack? He didn't get anxiety attacks!

Regardless, Trent's arrival that night had interrupted whatever Nick's mind was doing, and it had turned out to be a

Godsend. A distracted grin crossed Nick's face as he stared at his bedroom ceiling. Though he didn't tell Trent about that night, he later found out that Trent had sent messages out to their friends to pray. That man's intuition was next level.

Nick frowned. Why had Trent come over that evening? In Nick's shocked state, he hadn't thought to ask – he was just happy to have someone with him. He should ask Trent one day. Maybe an answer to these dreams lies somewhere in Trent's answer?

With a heavy sigh Nick looked at his bedside table clock. It read just after two a.m. He had to be up at five to start at six, but there was no way he would be getting back to sleep now. Maybe he'd go for a quick jog around the neighborhood?

With that thought in mind, Nick pulled on a fresh T-shirt, snagged yesterday's hoodie off the back of his desk chair, and left the room. Fresh air, a change of scenery, and some time with God would do him good.

CHAPTER TWO

The click of Nick securing his vest echoed in the empty locker room. In the quiet of his Sunday morning start he checked his kit, while last night's dream continued to hang in the back of his mind, tickling his conscious with anxiety about what he might see on the shift today.

Kit ready, Nick closed his locker with a loud clang. He had to get past that accident. Grabbing his take away coffee, he made his way down the quiet corridor to be briefed for today's shift.

"Ready for another day on the beat?" greeted Eddie Hastings, a fellow police officer coming off the graveyard shift. He fell into step beside Nick, their polished shoes squeaking on the linoleum floor as they walked. "Tell you mate, I'm ready for home."

"Tough night?" Nick felt his mouth hitch as he glanced over at Eddie – the guy was good value and usually found something funny in any situation they came across. Eddie yawned. "You could say that."

"Ah well, look alive for another ten minutes, then get outta here."

Just then the station P.A. system crackled into life and a cool, calm voice came over the airwaves. "All staff report to the Muster Room."

Nick and Eddie exchanged a look. When all staff were called, it only meant one thing – a big announcement was going to be made.

In the Muster Room, Nick placed his hat and diary at one of the tables and took his seat, while Eddie swung a chair around and sat facing Nick. "You off to see Alice after work?" Eddie wiggled his eyebrows and Nick dipped his head. "You need to get yourself a woman and stop asking about mine."

"Hey," Eddie held up his hands, feigning innocence. "I am looking. Any single gals in your…"

Just then Senior Sergeant Geoff Eldridge, the Field Training and Assessment Officer assigned to Nick at the Richmond Police Station, entered the room with the station's Inspector, Colin Hartford. Everyone fell silent and Eddie turned his seat to face the front. The hush that fell was tangible – it felt like being in first grade with the principal in the room.

Geoff sat heavily into a seat beside Nick, "Good morning. Ready for another day on the job?"

Geoff was shorter than Nick's six feet, and solidly built. With a no-nonsense attitude but an approachable smile, he had quickly earnt Nick's trust and loyalty, however, with the amount of hair on his forearms and his bushy eyebrows, it made Nick wonder – who was hairier, Geoff or Esau?

"Always ready, Sir."

Inspector Hartford called the room to order, and Geoff turned in his seat as Nick opened his diary ready to take notes. There was a seriousness in the inspector's expression that made the officers sit up straighter and caused the fine hairs on the back of Nick's neck to rise.

"Good morning, Officers. I'll get straight down to business. Some of you may have heard that a man recently detained for stalking others in the outer suburbs was released on bail this morning. His bail conditions, I'm informed, include that he is not to return to The Valley in particular, but we have reason to believe he will. Intel have informed us that during interrogation a link to the drug cartel we are after were revealed, but there is not enough evidence to detain him any longer."

Nick turned his pen end to end on the table as he listened, feeling his jaw clench. He knew who the Inspector was referring to. The stalker had visited two of his friends: Lexi Slaydon and Hope Meyer. At the time, he had assured them that the guy was not a threat – just an obsessed fan from their friend Dylan Saunders' professional football days. While Nick knew there was a team following the drugs case surrounding Dylan's brother, Jack, his hands had been tied with what he could do personally. He still felt a responsibility to protect his friends.

Nick shook his head. Jack was lucky to be alive. What started off as making poor friend choices while struggling with the death of his father, ended up with the kid running drugs and taking drugs himself. With no money to repay the debt he had accumulated, Jack's new 'friends' had come after him a couple of times – eventually landing Jack in hospital fighting for his life. Since then, Jack had been arrested and gone through rehab, but it was clear that the problems of the past hadn't completely gone away. Jack's family and friends were still under threat.

Nick stirred when a chair scraped on the linoleum floor beside him. He turned to see Geoff rising – the Inspector had finished his announcement and now it was time to get to work. Nick slipped his hat under his arm before joining the hand over conversation between Eddie and Geoff. Although he tried to focus on preparing for the day ahead, what he really wanted to do was find out more about this guy who had just been released. It sounded ominous. Where exactly had he been released to and why did they believe he would return to The Valley? What did he want? Was it because they couldn't reach Jack that they were going after those around him – using this guy?

A cold finger ran up Nick's spine. This went deeper than what he first believed. He needed to tell his friends.

He jumped slightly as a hand landed on his shoulder – he turned a carefully guarded expression to Geoff. "Let's hit the road, Nick, we have a number of papers to serve."

* * * *

"So where were you when we were doing hand over?"

Nick glanced at Geoff. The man's gaze was fixed on the road in front of them as they meandered their way around the city streets towards their first address to serve. "Sir?"

Geoff indicated around a slow driver. "You need to keep your mind on the job, son. It doesn't look good when an officer isn't focused on the day's duties – as mundane as they may be."

Disappointed in himself, Nick returned his attention to the road – they were only a few blocks away from the first address. He didn't want to appear as anything less than 100% focused on the job. "Sorry sir, I was distracted by hearing about that stalker being released on bail."

"Is he known to you?"

"He's known to my friends. I'm just concerned that he was released, and that the inspector thinks he'll return to The Valley."

The radio crackled into life, interrupting their conversation, and the no-nonsense voice of Erin from the Police Communications Centre spoke into their midst. "D24 Any unit attend Code 43."

Geoff picked up the handpiece. "Mount Vale 375 D24 received, go ahead."

"Residential fire. 402 White Cresent, Black Hill. Ambulance and Fire en route."

"Mount Vale 375 en route. Ten-four."

Geoff hung up the handpiece and dropped a gear in their high-performance Ford Falcon. The force pressed Nick back into the seat as he reached for the lights and sirens. A zip of adrenaline fired down his limbs and Nick punched in the address on the GPS. He was yet to attend a fire and couldn't deny a flutter of nerves filling his stomach at what he was about to see.

Traffic was congested on the narrow one-way street. Fenced town houses lined the street, and the nature strips were filling with people while smoke billowed from a house at the end. Geoff pulled their car in as close to the fire as practical and sent Nick off to establish a traffic cordon.

Thankful his job was only to direct traffic, Nick watched closely how Geoff dealt with worried neighbors and rubberneckers, while fire fighters hurried around calling out to each other. The fire hose blasted into action. A scream sounded above the hubbub and Nick whirled around. The fine hairs on the back of his neck stood on end while his eyes searched the gathered throngs. Geoff was dealing with it with firm but gentle hands – preventing a young man from running back into the building.

Nick turned from the scene as the crowd continued to grow, wondering what could be back inside that would drive someone to want to run into flames. The look on the man's face held both fear and determination as he tried to reason with Geoff to let him past. Whatever was inside, he was willing to risk his life for it.

With a prayer for protection over what or who was still inside the building, Nick forced his mind to refocus on the task at hand. Like Geoff said, he had to keep his mind on the job.

CHAPTER THREE

Nick strolled towards the leadlight-surrounded front entrance of his girlfriend Alice Knight's family home, when the door opened and she stepped out. Her long brunette hair, usually worn tightly in a bun, floated freely around her face in the afternoon breeze as she ambled towards him. "Officer Marshall."

A broad grin spread over Nick's face at her playful tone as he continued towards her. "I'll never tire of hearing you call me that."

Alice paused on her approach, as he closed the distance between them. "How's your weekend been so far?" She asked.

"Good. But I can think of one thing that would have made church better…" Linking his hands around her waist, Nick drew her in and kissed her. He felt Alice clasp the collar of his shirt. "We've been over this, I've told you why I won't go with you," her voice was soft as a purr against his mouth. "And I'm not a thing."

Nick grinned before kissing her again. Her arms came around his neck and the disappointed thoughts faded from his mind. He felt she was his equal in every way except the one that mattered most – though seeing Josh arrive at church with Hope yesterday, a minor miracle, reignited his anticipation that circumstances would change and Alice would attend church soon.

The sound of the front door opening and her mum leaving the house saw Alice disengage herself and swivel around within Nick's arms.

"Aren't you two out of the honeymoon phase, yet?" Mrs. Knight called as she moved towards the car parked in the driveway. Nick dropped his head to Alice's shoulder as she hugged his arms around her waist.

"Where are you off to?" Alice called out.

The sound of the car's alarm disengaging disturbed a flock of Long-billed Corellas in the towering eucalyptus trees and Nick raised his head to watch them take off, shrieking, into the sky.

"Going to grab pizzas for dinner. Dads got some news to share. I'll be back in ten."

Alice and Nick shuffled to the side of the driveway to avoid the car reversing past them. With a lift of his hand to Mrs. Knight, Nick felt his stomach rumble at the thought of pizzas – but if there was family business about to take place, maybe he should get going? Just then Alice turned and, linking her hands with his, began to walk backwards towards the house. "Wanna see what I've been working on?"

"Yeah. Lead away." Nick allowed Alice to pull him towards the house, pushing aside the thoughts that he should leave.

The Knight's home, set in the surrounding hills of Briardale, was covered with native scrub and sheltered by flowering Eucalyptus trees. The house had a log cabin feel with a warmth to match; every time Nick pulled into the driveway a sense of peace enveloped him. Alice turned and hurried around the side of the house towards the rear. Rounding the garage, Nick followed

Alice along the rear and stopped when she gestured with a flourish towards the back door.

"Hey, you've finished it." A surge of pride swelled through Nick as his gaze travelled the mosaic glass artwork Alice had been working on. It took a moment for him to take it all in. Side panels depicting rolling hills and local birdlife, with a sunrise above the door, Nick shook his head at the detail she had included. "This is incredible. Well done."

Nick looked at Alice as she came alongside him. Her eyes, framed by thick, natural lashes, gleamed as she admired her work. "Yeah, I'm pretty stoked."

"I think you've picked the wrong profession."

Alice gave a light shake of her head. "It's amazing what you can learn to do off YouTube. It bugged me that the front door had beautiful glass art but the back door was so drab. But now I'm done, I want to do more."

The door opened and Alice's younger sister stepped out. Her expression radiated warmth as her eyes fell upon them. "Hey Nick!"

"Sarah." Nick nodded before turning back to Alice. "Listen, I think I'd better take off. Sounds like you've got family stuff happening this afternoon." Alice took his hands and shook her head just as there was the sound of a car pulling up out the front of the house. "Oh no, stay. It'll be fine. Whatever Dad wants to tell us, you can hear too."

Alice's pout, and the swing of her hand in his, saw Nick's resolve crumble. He turned away to see Mrs. Knight rounding the side of the house, pizzas in hand. He could do with a slice or two. He looked back at Alice and gave a playful roll of his eyes. "Alright, you twisted my arm."

"Was it me? Or was it the pizzas?"

Before Nick could retort, Mr. Knight appeared along with Alice's older brother, Marcus. Stepping down the steps between the retaining wall from the native scrub looking backyard, they looked to be wrapping up a conversation. Sarah squealed and Nick looked back over to where she was. She had her mum in a tight embrace, and Nick exchanged a glance with Alice. Though her expression matched his, there was a definite energy in the air around them.

"Ok Dad." Alice let go of Nick's hand and open-palm gestured to her family. "What's going on? What's this big news? And Sarah, what are you squealing about?"

Mr. Knight chuckled as he and Marcus helped themselves to pizza and waved them over. A hiss of a carbonated drink being opened added to the bird calls around them as Mrs. Knight poured some soft drink into plastic cups, while Sarah held a pizza slice above her face and with eagerness, gulped down a long stretching piece of cheese. Whatever the news was, Sarah was elated; though there was a niggle of warning in Nick's mind as he watched the family interacting.

After what seemed like an exaggerated length of time, Nick watched Mr. Knight finish a slice of pizza before dusting his hands off and looking at Alice. Nick shot Alice a look. Wide eyed, she kept her questioning gaze square on her dad.

"Alright, miss. Keep your on-the-beat look for business hours." Mr. Knight chuckled into his drink. "The news is, we'll be moving. I've been given an incredible opportunity up north, including a house and car, and we'll be headed off next weekend to check out the place. You kids are welcome if you wish, but if all goes well, your mother and I are off within 60 days."

Nick looked at Alice. Her eyes were still locked on her dad, despite the excited chatter going on around them. "Hey." Nick gave her arm a light nudge with his elbow. When she turned to him, he lifted his shoulder. There was conflict within the depths of those beautiful brown eyes.

Would she go as well?

CHAPTER FOUR

Nick pushed open the doors of The Valley Gymnasium and made his way through to the weights room. The crisp, citrus scent that greeted him he knew was designed to invigorate those working out, and today he was glad it was there to lift his mood.

The afternoon with Alice's family had left him in a mood he couldn't yet quantify. Alice had objected to Nick leaving the family to themselves, claiming she wanted him to stay, but there was more they needed to discuss without him present. He'd driven away and headed to the gym, feeling heavy about what the days ahead would bring.

Sunday evenings were usually quiet in the weights room, so it was a perfect time to catch up with the boys – debrief their past week and prepare for the week ahead. As Nick approached, he could see Dylan and Trent through the glass doors already going through their work outs.

"Fellas." Nick entered the room and made his way over to his preferred exercise bike. Trent waved from where he was jogging on the treadmill and Dylan looked up from the pec deck. "G'day Mate," Dylan grunted as he pulled the pads together.

"You look like there is a lot on your mind, brother." Trent's words were seamless despite the pace he was going. Nick raised an eyebrow – that man was a machine.

Nick mounted a bike and, after setting the course, wasted no time getting stuck in. That he had a lot on his mind was an understatement. "Alice's folks are moving north within 60 days. I have a gut feeling Alice will go with them."

Nick sighed. Just saying the words out loud made it real – and the knowledge of what was to come hit home. Earlier, Nick had excused himself from the family gathering and headed to the gym – he hadn't wanted to talk to Alice until she'd had time to process the news. But now he was at the gym, all he wanted to do was go back and talk to Alice.

The sound of the weights on the pec deck clanged as Dylan rose from the bench. "That's tough, man. A lot can happen in two months though."

"Yeah." Nick puffed. While he understood that, he also knew he was a realist. Not interested in fluff and sugar-coating, he called things as he saw them – and in this instance, if your whole family moves, what are the chances of you staying behind? Slim to none.

The thump thump of Trent's steady jog filled the silence between them, while adding a bass beat to the music playing over the sound system. Nick zoned out, keeping his eyes on the screen in front of him, watching the marker move on the cycle program he'd chosen. Fifteen minutes to go. Time to think about something other than Alice.

His mind wandered back to seeing Hope's Boyfriend Josh at church yesterday, and he lifted his head to look at Dylan. "How about Josh coming to church yesterday? Didn't expect that."

Dylan grinned through the obvious strain he was putting his body under on the power tower. "Yeah. Was great. Who would have thought that stubborn fool would change." Out of all of them, Dylan knew Josh the best – they had been on the same footy team and friends for years. "I think Hope will still be smiling today."

"He's been prayed for, for a long time." Trent wound down his jog to a brisk walk. "Was terrific to see; both him coming to the Lord and the repair of their relationship."

"Gotta say, I'm impressed with how Hope has handled things over the last couple of months. Having other people question her faith, and then the changes she's made as a result." Nick leaned into the bike, straining against the uphill trajectory the course had taken. "Wasn't sure how that one was going to turn out. I thought maybe they'd break up for good. I certainly didn't see Josh coming to church as part of it."

"Me either." Dylan grunted as he lifted his knees to his chest.

"Some are quick to respond to the Holy Spirit, while others take more persistence from the prayer warriors. That's why we need to keep praying for each other, and those around us." Trent stepped down from the treadmill and headed for the weights. Nick watched him go while continuing the pace he'd set himself. He'd been praying for Alice to come to church with him, but now it might be that he won't see the answer to any of those prayers.

The bike next to him geared up, drawing Nick from his inward thoughts. Dylan had set a low intensity course and glanced at him. "Thinking about Alice?" Nick felt his bike easing up and he looked back at the computer screen on his bike. His course was almost finished and had moved into cool down mode. He sat back and rolled his shoulders out while continuing to pedal at the slower pace. "Yeah. Bit flat really."

"I can tell. Any more you wanna tell me?"

Nick gave a shake of his head. Maybe if there weren't others in the room with them, he'd consider putting thoughts to words, but not tonight. He was still trying to anchor his thoughts in the knowledge that whatever happened, God knew what He was doing and it was for Nick's good and God's glory. "How's Jack doing?"

Out the corner of his eye, Nick could see Dylan drop his head. The delay in answer told him this was a hard topic for Dylan to talk about. As long as they'd been friends, Nick had always admired the resilience his mate seemed to have. No matter what hit him, he continued to hold others up around him and somehow pull himself up as well. But right now, it must be incredibly hard for him. Reaching over, Nick gave Dylan's shoulder a slap. "Hey, if you don't want to talk about him, that's ok."

"It's not that. He's stable. It's just everything around it." Dylan's hands dropped from the bike's handlebars and rested on his thighs as he peddled. "Jack's full of apologies – I think the penny has finally dropped with him, but Mum's a mess. There is security all around the house, police coming and going, and to make matters worse we've just been notified that the guy who was stalking me has been released."

Nick kept his eyes on the screen in front of him, watching the countdown timer. "Yeah, I just found out too. Sorry to hear, man."

"I don't know what to do. Sure, we can 'disappear' until the trial, but I know family and friends become targets if these people cannot get the person they're after. What's that mean for Mum? Mum's brother Uncle Shane? You guys?"

Dylan's words faded off, and Nick glanced at him. Even if the trial saw Jack locked up, he could still be a target in prison. The crowd he got himself in with want their money; bottom line. "Look, D, we all know worrying won't get you anywhere. We're closing in on the crowd who are after Jack, so you just gotta hang tight. It's a waiting and faith game this."

Spontaneous laughter broke out in the room and Nick looked over to see some older men who had come in, sharing a laugh as they put the dumbbells away. An odd paradox. Shouldn't it be him and his friends laughing, and the older men sharing worries? The bike course ceased, and Nick stopped peddling. "I'll see what I can find out tomorrow to ease your worries brother ok?"

"I'd appreciate that." Dylan looked over at him. "Thanks."

CHAPTER FIVE

*H*ope's car was already parked out the front of Youth Minister Dave Thomas' house when Nick pulled up. He grinned as he shifted his Clubsport into neutral and killed the engine. She'd come a long way recently; changed a lot about herself to reflect what she believed, and God had blessed her. He was proud of his friend.

With a few quick strides, Nick reached the landing and the front door opened before him. Dave's wife, Linda, greeted him with a warm smile. "Evening Nick, how's your day been?" She stepped back, motioning for him to enter.

Nick gave a dip of his head as he passed by her, "Do you really wanna know?"

"By that answer, I'm going to say no." Linda gave a soft chuckle and closed the door behind them. "Go on through. Dave's just on the phone, he'll join you shortly."

Laughter greeted Nick as he opened the door to Dave's library. Lexi was mid story about something that happened at the café earlier that day, and he listened as he crossed the cozy room to take his normal seat on the church pew under the window next to Dylan.

"So, when did you realize that was happening?" Dylan's face held a mix of endearment and skepticism. Lexi tried to reign in a giggle so that she could answer Dylan's question, but Hope beat her to it. "I'm going to take a wild guess and say when she saw the chips raining down from the third-floor balcony!"

Lexi snorted and covered her reddening face with her hand, as another wave of laugher shook her body. Dylan rolled his eyes and shrugged. "Kids."

"I've missed something." Nick's tone was cautious as he watched Hope and Lexi try to contain their laughter. "What happened today?"

Dylan replied, "just some kids fooling around in the third-floor food court. They were throwing chips over the balcony and one landed in the drink of a well-to-do patron. He got rather animated from what I can gather. He jumped back, knocked his chair over, splashing more of his drink. Shook his fist at the kids... it was chaos."

Just then the library door opened and Dave entered, followed by Trent. "Thanks for coming everyone. Sorry that phone call took a bit longer than I thought." The chatter settled down and murmurs greeted Dave as he moved through the room to sit behind his desk. While watching his youth minister's movements through the room, Nick caught Hope looking at Trent. It was the type of look you'd give someone if you were seeing them for the first time. Curious, Nick feigned a yawn and glanced around the room as he crossed his arms. If Trent was aware of Hope's perusal, he had not let on. Tucking the exchange away in his mind, and knowing the change within Hope and that her relationship with

Josh was back on track, Nick was intrigued as to what he glimpsed in her expression.

When Nick focused back on the meeting, Icebreaker ideas were being thrown around the room. While he enjoyed all the ideas, he found himself most drawn to the suggestion of free play – by Friday he was mentally exhausted. Some weeks when he turned up for youth night he knew he was only there in body, so the idea of free play, with Dave taking the message, was like a night off. The vote passed – all in favor of free play. Perfect.

Movement across the room drew his attention to Hope, who had sat forward on her seat and clasped her hands together, as if that action could contain whatever was about to burst from her. "Ok guys, now that's sorted I *have* to share some news!"

Lexi turned to her and laid a hand on her arm. "Is it...?"

"Yes!" Hope gave a rapid nod of her head. "I got the job with Adventist Volunteers!"

All at once they were on their feet in celebration. Hope's laugh ran out over the chatter of congratulations and questions until Dave clapped his hands. "Alright all, let's give Hope the floor to share this news with us."

"Thanks Dave." Hope retook the edge of her seat and drew in a long breath through her beaming smile. "Ok. So, I start next week – sorry Dave, I'll be an apology for next Monday."

"That's understandable, Hope. Go on." Dave gave a dip of his head.

"And I'll be gone for a week and I'm just over the moon about it. I cannot wait to get on that plane and fly out to this remote little country church and help set up for their evangelistic meeting coming up. It all seems so surreal!" Hope let out a little squeal as she finished speaking and Nick couldn't help the smile that broke out upon his face. Lexi plopped onto the seat next to Hope and embraced her as Dylan asked another question. Nick noticed Trent sat back in his seat with an enigmatic grin on his face as he watched on.

Whatever that exchange was between Hope and Trent this evening, it had blinked on his radar, and confidence tipped the corner of his mouth as he steadily regarded Trent.

He'd find out what was going on.

And soon.

CHAPTER SIX

*N*ick strode through the corridors of the Richmond Police Station looking for Detective Wayne Brooks. One question was burning in his mind: what was the latest news with Jack?

Dylan was right. Even if Jack was out of the way, that just shifted the goons' target onto Jack's family and friends. Like it or not, this case involved Nick. He sighed as he entered the detective's office. The large space felt like a living area of a well-to-do home. Detective Brooks looked up from his computer.

"Nick Marshall. What brings you around?"

Nick pulled the leather swivel chair out and tentatively sat down. He knew there were protocols surrounding what information could be made available to him, but he thought he'd try his luck. "Good morning, Sir. I'm looking for an update on the Jack Saunders case."

A sigh answered Nick's question as the detective sat back in his chair. Two double hung windows spilt the morning sun around him, giving him a rosy silhouette that was the opposite to the coolness Nick sensed coming from him. "Nick. We've spoken about this. I cannot give you any more details than already divulged. Why are you asking again?"

"Yes, Sir. I understand. However, in the wake of this latest hit on Jack I am becoming increasingly concerned about those around me who know him. Also, the release of the stalker who'd been hanging around The Valley reportedly looking for Dylan, is he connected in some way?"

Detective Brooks held up his hands. "Your concerns have been noted, Nick. However, my hands are tied."

Frustration nipped at Nick's conscious. He knew where his superior was coming from, but he still hoped for a special favor. He sat forward on the seat. "Ok. Can you tell me anything at all about the stalker? Are he and Jack linked in anyway?"

"That, we are still ascertaining."

"Has there been a team assigned to monitor him? The Inspector believes he will return to The Valley. Why would he do that if he's not in some way connected to what happened with the Saunders family?"

Just then there was a knock on the office door and Detective Brooks rose to his feet, gesturing for whoever was behind Nick to enter. Glancing back at him, the detective wrapped up. "Nick – as earlier stated, your concerns have been noted. If anything changes, you'll be notified."

Understanding that was his cue, Nick rose and thanked the detective for his time before acknowledging his colleague who had entered the room. He left the office, careful not to bang the door with frustration behind him.

No further enlightened as to what was happening, Nick made his way back to his desk and decided to bury himself in the paperwork that was mounting. Every phone call and every time he stepped out of the office required a paper trail. It was exhausting, but at least he could turn his mind off from the trouble he sensed was knocking on his door.

* * * *

The early summer evening was perfect. A lingering sunset sent splashes of violet, amber, gold and vibrant pinks across the sky, reflecting over the rippling, licorice water. "So, tell me." Nick held Alice's hand as they strolled the main beach at dusk. "How did the family meeting end up the other night?"

He couldn't imagine The Valley without Alice and prayed he'd never have to. Looking down, feeling her fingers caress his, he waited for her reply. At her soft sigh, he paused their stroll and took her other hand. "Whatever it is, you can tell me."

Her gaze continued downward for a moment before lifting to look along the sand from where they'd come. "It's hard to imagine my whole family will be gone from here within two months." Alice looked up at Nick. "I don't know if I could stay here knowing they were so far away."

Thoughts crashed into Nick's mind in an unrelenting torrent. Should he try to convince her to stay? Should he encourage her to go? Could they handle a long-distance relationship or was he looking at a breakup? "You thinking of going?"

Alice gave a slight nod of her head. Her darkened eyes appeared all the darker as if reflecting the depth of her struggle with her decisions. "I spoke to my Field Training and Assessment Officer about a transfer to a Police station up North. She's going to look into it. Nothing formal, just making enquiries at this stage."

Her voice was faraway and her shoulders slumped. Despite the crushing sensation within his chest, Nick drew her into his arms and rested his cheek against the top of her head. Her arms linked low around his waist as she rested her head against his chest. "I'm so sorry Nick."

Surprised, Nick felt his eyebrows jump as he looked over the darkening sun set. "What for? I know how close you are to your family."

Alice drew her head back and looked up at him. "Yeah, but what about us?"

"If you're not sold on moving, then stay. Get a rental and tough it out for six months to a year. If you don't like it, then go?" Nick ran his hands over her silken hair. "At least then you'll have tried the options before you and can make a final decision."

"If I go, do you think we'll last?" Alice's voice was like a whisper as she hugged herself closer to Nick. His body warmed in response, and he looked over her head at the last thread of gold along the horizon. A smile spread over his face. "Where there is a will there is a way."

"There's a definite will here."

There was a certainty about the tone of Alice's voice which quieted the worry in Nick's mind. He looked back at her. Her lips glistened in the rising moonlight as she smiled back at him; he knew she didn't want to go, but he knew how tight the family were. He'd not make this decision harder for her. Dipping his head, Nick kissed her lightly.

Two months was a long time and anything could happen. However, for the moment she seemed open to the option of renting in the area, and that was enough for him. In her arms, worries faded from his awareness and the future looked promising.

"Wanna have a look around at some rentals during the week?" Nick felt the roughened note in his voice and cleared his throat. The corner of Alice's mouth hitched, and a mischievous gleam twinkled in her eyes. "Could be a bit of fun. Sure."

"One day at a time." Nick brushed a strand of hair back from Alice's face and tucked it behind her ear. She leaned into his touch. "One day at a time."

CHAPTER SEVEN

Nick made his way inside the church hall. He knew Dylan and Lexi had already arrived. However, the hall was quiet. Perhaps they were setting up for café? A door opened at the far end of the hall, it's woody creak alerting Nick of someone's entrance, and Dave came into view. He was distracted, looking down at the phone in his hand.

"G'day Dave." Nick strolled towards his youth minister. Dave looked up as he pocketed his phone. "Nick. Great to see you." Dave stopped before him. "Good week?"

Nick bobbed his head. "Yeah, not bad. Where are the others?"

Just then Lexi's laughter spilled into the hall from the kitchen and Nick turned. Lexi was looking over her shoulder back at Dylan who reached out to her, but she leapt away with a yelp and a giggle. Nick couldn't help but grin as he observed them. He'd watched Dylan hide his feelings for Lexi for such a long time, and now it was hard to imagine them ever not being a couple.

"Hey Nick!" Lexi called out as she picked up a bag of items from the floor. "Come and see what I've brought for tonight's free play." Feeling a rap on his shoulder, Nick glanced at Dave who waved him off. "You go, I've got a few things to finish up before we start. I'll be in my office – keep an eye on the clock, the youth will arrive in fifteen minutes."

By the time Nick crossed the hall, Lexi had emptied out a sack of dress-up items. He frowned as he came to a stop before her. The hall door opened beside him, and he glanced to his right to see Hope shrugging off a lightweight jacket. Her eyes were glued to the things Lexi was laying out against the wall. "Is that what I think it is?"

Lexi jumped excitedly. "I couldn't help it. A school I was speaking at today was clearing out and updating their drama room costumes, and wanted all this gone. So of course I offered to take it." Nick watched Hope trot over to the pile of swords, shields, light sabers, capes, spy glasses, hats, sheriff badges, gowns, shoes, masks; her eyes alight and mouth wide open. This was right up her alley.

With a shake of his head, Nick moved towards Dylan, avoiding the girls as they discussed the fun the youth would have with the donated gear. "Evening, Dylan."

"Nick."

"I thought tonight would be more ball games type of free play. What is this?"

"This, is what's commonly called fun," Dylan chuckled. "C'mon, let's see if we can find you something that won't embarrass you."

Nick watched Dylan move towards the girls and join them in going through the items Lexi had brought. Fun. Ok.

Begrudgingly, he moved to join his friends. There was no getting out of it, and the youth would be here soon expecting him to play. He glanced at the clock just as Lexi jumped into his line of sight; a shield in her left hand and what looked like a light saber in her right. "En garde, you!"

Nick remained unmoved at her cheeky jabs around his waist, her eyes wide and playful as she goaded him into parry. To his side he heard Dylan make a sound of challenge while his peripheral picked up Hope rising to her feet. A grin began to curl on Lexi's face and Nick could tell she was becoming emboldened by his lack of movement to her advances. If he was reading her right, the next move would be higher and bolder. There was a slight tensing of her body, moments before the lunge came. In a heartbeat he was back in self-defense training. Stepping into her lunge, Nick grasped her wrist with his right hand while his left closed over the handle of the saber. Laughter bubbled out of Lexi as the shield she held clattered to the ground while she employed the use of her other hand to keep hold of the saber. Caught up in the playfulness of the moment, Nick broke into a grin as he gave her wrist a quick tweak and then chuckled as the saber rattled to the floor.

A cheer sounded from somewhere in the room as Nick shared a laugh with Lexi. But a flicker behind her eyes alerted him to something amiss. Her jovial expression dissolved and he felt a weak tug of her arm under the grip he had on her wrist. Realizing he still had hold of her, Nick released his grip while reading the ever-changing expressions on his friend's face. What felt like minutes he knew had only been seconds, but Lexi's rosy glow had paled and her widened eyes stared back at him for a moment before she turned and fled from the hall.

CHAPTER EIGHT

Nick stepped out into the gentle warmth of the night and looked for Lexi. After she'd left the hall in such a hurry, the young people had begun to enter and they'd wasted no time in grabbing the props and joining Dylan and Hope in impromptu games. Nick had not missed the protective stare of Dylan's in the direction Lexi had exited as the youths vied for his attention. Nick had indicated to Dylan that he'd sort it out, and although Dylan's mouth had thinned, he gave a slight nod of his head.

Lexi was seated on a bench against the side wall of the church building, head lowered and hands clenched in her lap. Nick closed the door behind him, shutting the ruckus from the hall out from the peaceful garden, and approached her. "How you doing, champ?"

Lexi looked up, took a long deep breath and blew it out. "I'm so sorry."

Nick rested a hip against one of the verandah posts opposite where she sat and crossed his arms. "Wanna talk about it?"

"I just feel so silly. I mean, it's you."

A frown crossed Nick's brow as he considered what she had said. Something had happened in their playful sparring match that had led to Lexi fleeing the hall quicker than he'd seen her move before. He just wasn't sure what it was – she'd started the game.

Lexi sighed softly, her gaze taking in the garden around them. "Sometimes there's an obvious trigger, but other times it just hits me. Blindsides me completely and I just need a moment. Like when we were playing around in there…" Lexi stopped and looked at her clasped hands. "All it took was when you grasped my wrists. Suddenly I was back to when…" She raised a hand to her mouth as her voice broke.

Realization dawned and Nick pushed himself off the post and moved to sit beside her. He knew Lexi was talking about when her ex- boyfriend Brad had assaulted her in her home. Thankfully Nick had walked in just at the right moment, but it hadn't been the only time Brad was violent towards her.

"Yeah," Nick sighed heavily as he lowered himself onto the bench beside her. "I remember."

Just that memory of what he'd seen caused Nick's adrenaline to fire and he felt his jaw clench. He'd known Brad was bad news the moment he'd met him, and everyone had been happy to see the back of him. But the scars the guy had left on his friend were hard for Nick to move past. He turned to look at Lexi. Her eyes were closed and she sat stiffly. "Will you be ok in there tonight, Lexi?"

She gave a nod of her head before looking back at him. The darkness in her eyes was gone and the color was back in her face, though he didn't believe the smile she wore. He raised an eyebrow and she nodded again. "I'm ok. I just needed a moment. Promise."

The hall door opened and Dylan approached the two of them. With an unspoken exchange, Nick rose and clapped Dylan on the shoulder as he passed heading back into the hall.

The mood inside the hall was the opposite of what he'd just left outside, and he strolled towards the youth café while watching the youths continue playing with the props. Laughter was loud and the energy within the hall was electric, but he wasn't in the mood for dress ups. So, he began unstacking chairs for the café, hoping to avoid being drawn into any games.

"Hey, you. How's Lex?"

Nick looked over at Hope nearby and saw her starting to unstack chairs alongside him. "She's ok, Dylan's with her now."

"Those flashbacks are terrible." Hope gave a slow shake of her head as she tucked chairs under the table. "At least they are happening less often."

Nick slid some chairs under the table Hope was working at as a swell of anger against Brad rose again within him. At the time, when he'd busted Brad assaulting Lexi, it'd taken every ounce of his training at the Academy to restrain himself from giving Brad a bit of his own. "Maybe they're less often, but the intensity is still the same from what I saw."

Nick followed Hope as she moved away to the next table. Lexi aside, there was something he wanted to discuss with Hope, and this was as good a time as any. "So, tell me. What are you and Trent scheming for tonight?"

Hope pulled a chair off the stack and cast him a look filled with curiosity and confusion. "Nothing as far as I know. Why?"

"Did I catch something between you two on Monday night, while the chip fiasco at the Ocean View Café was being re-experienced?" Nick could feel Hope's eyes upon him and he gave a nonchalant glance at her. She pushed a chair under the table, her expression turning stony. "Are you serious?"

"You tell me."

A sharp exhale met his question and he watched Hope march to the stack of chairs, lift off two more and bring them back to the table. She didn't say anything, but he could sense she was reluctant to answer him. He decided to push her for an answer anyway. "Well?"

Hope looked up at him. There was a myriad of thoughts reflecting in her eyes that drew a raised eyebrow from Nick. "Does Josh know about this?"

"Are you both joining us tonight?" Trent's voice sounded behind Nick and he saw Hope jump, moments before a smile illuminated her face and she straightened. She looked past him, to Trent. "You bet! We're just about finished sorting the café out. Aren't we Nick?"

Nick's mouth curled as he looked from Hope to Trent then chuckled as he brushed a hand over the table. "Yep. All done here."

"Excellent." Trent said. "Lexi and Dylan are back and Dave's ready to start the message."

Nick watched as Hope moved away from the café towards the gathering youths. As she passed Trent, Nick caught sight of the bandage on the man's left hand. He looked at Trent. He had an impenetrable look about him as he met and held his stare. Nick gestured to his hand. "What happened to you?"

"Nail gun got me."

Nick grimaced as he began leaving the café area with Trent. "You'll be right tonight?"

Trent gave a nod of his head. "Yeah. It's not as bad as it sounds. The foreman sent me to the docs as a precaution, but Doctor says I'll be fine to go back to work on Monday."

Though Nick deflected the conversation off whatever was going on between Hope and Trent, it didn't take his mind off whatever was going on behind the scenes, sure had his interest now.

CHAPTER NINE

"Hey man."

Nick looked up from his work at the sound of his colleague's voice. He put his pen down and stretched out his fingers before linking them behind his head. "Hey Eddie."

"Big morning, I hear." Eddie took a seat on the edge of Nick's desk and pinched a mint from his mint jar. Nick yawned and nodded. "It was intense."

Eddie gave a wry smile as he crossed his arms. "Yeah, I've had a few like that."

Nick lowered his arms and tilted his coffee mug towards him before taking a sip of the remaining caramel-colored liquid. It had cooled and Nick scowled, swallowing it with effort. "I need a refill. How's the afternoon shift looking?"

"Got some papers to serve and attend a prisoner transfer…"

Nick rose and speared off from his cubical towards the kitchen. "Walk and talk."

Eddie cleared his throat. "...then it's paperwork until home time, unless we get called out. Did you hear about Johnson's experience with a prisoner transfer?"

The soft tap tap of keyboards and the murmurs of hushed conversations filled the air as they walked. Nick glanced at Eddie. "Johnson? Is he out of hospital yet?"

"They're going to run a few more tests, like for hepatitis, AIDS and all that, change his dressing, then he can go. But I tell ya..."

"Don't you start worrying about being bitten." Nick put his mug on the kitchen counter and after selecting a double-shot coffee pod, dropped it into the coffee machine. "What happened to Johnson was a freak accident."

When Eddie didn't respond, Nick turned his eyes from his mug to Eddie. The man was leaning against the bench, looking out the door they'd just come through back into the office. Something else was on his mind. Nick crossed the small kitchen to the fridge for the milk. "Out with it. What's really going on."

A grunt met Nick's question, and he chuckled as he shut the fridge before heading back to the bench. Eddie was rubbing his forehead. "My house mate is moving out. I need to find another to take his place otherwise rent will kill me."

Nick gave a nod. He knew what the rent costs were, and it was one of the big reasons he'd chosen to remain at home a little longer than he wished. Ideally, he'd continue to save until he had enough to put a deposit on buying his first home, but it was starting to chafe being almost twenty-three and still at home.

Just then more officers entered the kitchen to make drinks and after exchanging pleasantries with them, Nick and Eddie headed back to their desks.

The coffee was perfect, and Nick took a couple of long gulps, relishing the bitter warmth that lined his mouth before slipping down his throat to pool satisfyingly in his stomach. An elbow in his side shattered his blissful reverie and he glared at Eddie just as he retook his seat. "You're lucky I didn't spill this, mate."

Eddie masked his laugh in a cough. "It's just a coffee. I gather you were too wrapped up in the moment with your drink to hear what I said?"

Nick gave a shake of his head, then took another mouthful of his drink.

"I said." Eddie rested a hip against Nick's cubical and crossed his arms. "Why don't you move in with me? You know, cut the umbilical cord with home?"

Nick chuckled, ignoring the umbilical cord comment. "I'm saving for a deposit to buy my own home. If I continue saving at the rate I am, I should have enough in 18 months – interest rates being the only variable in the plan."

"Well, rejig your figures and move in with me. It'd be great. We know each other, we understand each other – we're *normal*. Think about it… Anyway, I better get back to my desk."

With a shake of his head, Nick turned his attention back to the paperwork before him and yawned. Move in with Eddie? He'd only known the guy for six months or so. He gulped down the rest of his coffee and focused his mind back to finish the work before him – he'd think about Eddie later. Although, it was sounding appealing already.

CHAPTER TEN

"Happy birthday handsome, how has your day been?"

Nick eyed Alice over the intimate table setting, overlooking the lights of the city. She was resting her heart shaped face on the back of her hand and looking back at him through the candlelight. Her brunette hair was like rich liquid chocolate and it framed her face, curling under her jaw in long layers past her shoulders. Her doe brown eyes smiled at him through the choppy fringe in front of them. She wasn't wearing her glasses for their date tonight which made her eyes look larger and revealed how long her lashes were. As he gazed back at her, she began to lightly run the back of her fingers along the length of her jaw, drawing his eyes to her mouth. He knew what she was doing, but it still worked and he grinned back at her – he could look at her all day. He cleared his throat. "My day. Ehm, it was good. Yours?"

"Oh, I was thinking about you."

"Really?" Nick leaned forward. Slipping his hand under hers, he removed the distracting fingers close to her mouth and held her hand over the tabletop so he could concentrate. "You were thinking about me? In what way?"

"Well, I know we were going to have a look at some rentals together this week, but there was one advertised at work…"

Alice looked down at their hands before placing her other hand over the top and looking back at him. "I went to see it, and it's really cute. I think you'd like it too."

It was in the way she held his gaze, that he knew the subtext of what she was saying. He returned her cheeky smile as he straightened. Alice's eyes flickered, as she leant forward towards him. "It's between both our works. Off-road parking. High fencing – you can have that dog you've always been talking about."

Nick drew in a breath and chuckled as he settled back in his chair. He needed to slow this train down. "You're thinking that we move in together?"

"Well, yeah." Alice's voice held a trepidation which Nick steeled himself against. He didn't want to hurt her, but he did not believe in cohabiting before marriage. Withdrawing his hands from hers, Nick pulled his chair around the table to sit closer to her. "When we spoke about you leaving or staying, I said that I'd come with you to look for rentals – I meant rentals for you, not the both of us."

Alice searched his eyes for a moment before dropping her head – her face became covered by the shimmering drape of her hair. Nick could hear her self-depreciating sniff and saw the slight shake of her head before she looked back up, sending her hair rippling over her shoulders. The smile she wore belied the foolishness she felt. "Oh, I feel so stupid. I misread that conversation completely."

Nick smiled at the lightness in her voice and ran his thumb over the back of her hand. "Easy to do. It could have been taken both ways."

The tinkle of cutlery, the hushed conversations and music playing softly in the background filled the silence between them while Alice looked like she wanted to ask something. Nick gave her room to voice what was on her mind while he picked up his glass and took a sip of the sparkling water. Alice straightened. "Would you consider it, though?"

Nick replaced his glass and turned back to her. "Move in with you?"

"Yeah."

He knew their relationship had been headed towards this conversation for a while, and now here it was. With a quick prayer for his words and intention to be understood, he cleared his throat. "Marry you? Yes. I have considered that for some time. Move in with you before marriage? No."

An alluring blush spread over Alice's cheeks as she coyly grinned back at him. It'd been the first time he'd voiced the idea of marriage to her and, by the look of her response, she wasn't averse to the idea. She tucked a strand of hair behind an ear. "So why not move in together then? It'd be fun."

Nick sighed. "I'm sure it would be. But I don't go with the 'try before you buy' mentality of society."

There was a subtle guarding of her expression which Nick didn't miss. There had been a few topics they had different opinions on – which he hadn't decided were deal-breakers or not – and it looked like they were now going to work through another major one.

Alice wriggled back in her seat and took a sip from her drink. "I wouldn't have picked you as the really old-fashioned type, Officer Marshall." Nick raised his eyebrows in response. "I didn't think I'd given you much reason to suspect otherwise."

"Just stirring." Alice lent forward and brushed Nick's leg under the table, then sat back in her chair once again. "So, tell me about these archaic thoughts of yours. Is this a Christian thing to not live with someone before marriage? 'Cos I know plenty of Christians who do."

Nick drew a long breath in through his nose and released it slowly. The problem that arises when people decide to compromise on truths is that it leads others astray. "Yes. I do too." Nick ran a hand through his hair while thinking about how best to rebut her well-ingrained ideology. While a part of him didn't want to dive into it, he sensed God was opening a door for him to speak with Alice about his faith. "There is a consistent theme through the Bible that a man and woman are to leave their respective families and become one flesh together. This means marriage. Not to see if they like or love each other enough to give marriage a go." Watching Alice closely, Nick lent forward – praying she was listening and not just humoring him. "It's a whole heart commitment. God takes marriage seriously and everything that goes with it. So do I."

A moment passed before Alice gave a nod of her head. She was no doubt thinking over what he'd said and applying that to her picture of their future. "That's a firm no to moving in, then, isn't it?"

Nick shifted in his seat. Was this a deal-breaker for her? She seemed relaxed as she looked back at him, "Yes," he replied.

"That's ok. I respect you for that. I have a couple of girlfriends I could ask to move in with me." Alice reached for her glass and drew it to her. "Just one thing, though, if it's a teaching from the Bible, why do some Christians do the whole living together thing before marriage?"

Nick chuckled as he reached for his glass. "Very good question. Why do any of us not do what we've been asked? If people always did what they've been asked, then we wouldn't have the jobs that we have!" Nick let that sit for a moment while he downed the rest of his drink, then he turned back to Alice. She looked as if she was considering how to answer, but when her mouth opened and nothing but an exhale came out – along with a raised shoulder – Nick continued. "God gives us sound guidelines on how to live and to look after our bodies, but it's up to us if we want to follow them. Bottom line, when it comes to cohabitation, statistics show that higher divorce rates come from couples who have lived together before getting married. God knows best. I choose to believe this and follow His way of living."

"Is that why you don't drink too?" Alice gave a nod towards his glass of sparkling water.

Nick grinned. "It's one of the many reasons why I don't drink. And God has helped me to quit swearing, too, even though it can be hard being around some of the guys at work and not letting their words get in my head."

Alice pushed her empty plate aside. Nick could see she really was considering what he had said. Up until this evening, topics around his beliefs had been skimmed over and Nick had thought she wasn't interested in how his faith influenced the decisions he made. But tonight, her questions had gone deeper. Perhaps his numerous prayers for her were beginning to see doors open?

As the waiter reappeared and collected up their plates and Nick waved off the offer for more drinks, a lightness entered his mind. He knew God heard every prayer, and he knew God's timing was perfect. For a moment, he had thought that Alice's family leaving meant the end of their relationship, but now she was looking at rentals so she could stay, and she was even asking some tough but good questions.

Did this mean she was in it for the long haul?

That assurance would be the best present ever.

CHAPTER ELEVEN

*N*ick ambled through the Bridgeshore Plaza, looking for the shop whose name was on the gift card in his back pocket. Soulway. He hadn't heard of this shop before – then again, he didn't visit the Plaza often. Most of the shopping he did for himself was along Main Street at the surf shops. However, his parents must think it was time to change his look.

He almost walked right past Soulway – it was as small as the kitchen at his house. Skeptical, Nick pursed his lips as he gazed at the items in the shop window. Cotton jeans, natural-colored shirts, straw hats, loafers – was Boho the best way to describe this shop? Maybe he would just re-gift the gift card?

"Hello there. Can I help you?"

Nick turned at the voice next to him. A young man, not more than seventeen years old, stood in the doorway looking at him expectantly. He was dressed identical to the mannequin in the window. With great effort, Nick pushed down the urge to decline the polite request, and decided to give the young man a chance.

Twenty minutes later, Nick stood in the change room eyeing himself in the mirror. Camel-colored suede pants, kangaroo leather woven belt and a light blue shirt with the top two buttons undone. Finished off with a navy blazer and a pair of loafers. A far cry from his normal casualwear, but he kind of liked it. Even the loafers. Surprisingly.

With the assessment of his appearance finished, Nick turned to exit the change room. As his eyes grazed over the top of the louvered door and out into the Plaza beyond, a figure drew his eye. He paused. Something was familiar about that trench coat and sunglasses, the searching head movements and the way they were walking. They reminded him of someone he was hoping never to see again.

Nick's keen eyes watched the figure as it moved slowly through the throngs of people headed for the escalators, leading to the second floor.

The Ocean View Café was on the second floor.

Where Lexi worked.

He had to call the station.

* * * *

"Whoo hoo. Look at you."

Lexi's face was lit up like the Christmas lights that were beginning to line the Plaza as she moved towards the counter of the Ocean View Café. Nick gave a droll grin as he sat astride a stool, tapping one foot against the other leg. "Thanks Lexi. I had a birthday voucher to spend. But look…"

"Hey Trent, get a look at Nick here." Lexi interrupted.

A frown crossed Nick's brow as Lexi turned away. Nodding at Trent, who was seated at the other end of the counter, she went to serve another customer. A moment later, Trent shuffled closer, raising the cup of tea in his hand in salute. "Looking good, brother."

With a roll of his eyes, Nick readjusted the neckline of the blazer he wore. "No work today?"

"Finished early. Now have a couple days off until the next contract starts."

Lexi returned and Nick leaned forward. He locked his gaze on her, trying to convey the urgency he felt, until he had her full attention. Keeping his voice hushed, Nick spoke. "That guy who visited both yourself and Hope..." The smile on Lexi's face fell away as she pulled the tea towel off her shoulder and stepped up closer to the counter. "Is he in the Plaza?" Her lowered voice held a tremor and, in his peripheral, Nick caught Trent straighten on the stool and turn to look behind them.

Nick gave a nod of his head at Lexi's question. "I've called it in to work, and they're sending officers around to arrest him on the grounds of breaking bail conditions. I just wanted to give you a heads up in case he comes by here."

Lexi nodded her head rapidly. Her eyes darted between him and Trent. "Ok. Um, hey... I finish work in half an hour. Do you have anything else to do around here? Can you stick around? Wouldn't mind someone to walk me back to my car, is all."

The anxiety within Lexi was tangible. Her eyes were wide and the way her fingers now clenched the tea towel in her hands made the audible request for an escort through the car park unnecessary. Trent laid a hand over hers. Nick glanced at the gesture before looking back at her. "Sure. I can hang around here with Trent and keep an eye out."

"Thanks guys. I appreciate that." Lexi stood up straighter and glanced over her shoulder at the coffee machine. "Can I get you anything?"

"Got something to match this outfit?" Nick shot Lexi a grin, hoping the derisive remark about himself would help her relax. A moment passed before a smile broke out on her face, followed by a soft giggle as she turned away to face the coffee machines. "I do. Give me a sec."

Just then a sharp buzz broke into the din and Nick snatched his phone from his rear pocket. He drew it to his ear. "Yeah. Nick here."

"We got him. He's back in custody." The no-nonsense voice of one of his coworkers barked down the line. "Thanks for the tip."

Nick's breath rushed out as relief flooded his body. "Thanks."

The call disconnected and Nick relaxed back in his seat. Lexi stood at the counter looking back at him, a hopeful expression upon her face. A slight nod of his head and his smile made her face illuminate as she turned her attention back to the task she was working on.

But Nick was still concerned; sure, the guy was about to be back behind bars, but for how long? And why had he come back to The Valley? Nick turned to Trent and found his piercing eyes locked on him. In the silent exchange that followed, he felt an odd sensation like a prickling over his skin.

Did Trent know something? His intuition told him he did. Now was not the time to draw it from him though.

This was not over.

* * * *

Nick strode into his workplace and made his way straight to Detective Wayne Brooks' office. The door was open, and Nick could see the man was on the phone. Nick gave a light tap on the open door and the detective motioned for him to enter and sit. Becoming aware of his bouncing leg the longer that the phone call continued, Nick pushed a hand down on his knee. Although the bouncing stopped, he could now feel his muscles twitching. Prayers for calm and clarity filled his mind as he turned to look out the office window.

Trent's gaze had resonated somewhere deep inside of him. In that moment he had felt insignificant and yet comforted by the awareness of things beyond himself. Although he'd maintained his impenetrable façade, his intuition told him that Trent had seen right through it. But for what purpose? What was Trent looking for within Nick? Or was Trent trying to tell him something? Nick knew he had always been good at reading people, but he couldn't read Trent this time. He felt blocked.

That fact unnerved him too.

Trent had left the café moments later, and Nick had found it hard to refocus his mind. It wasn't until Lexi tapped his arm ready to leave that he was able to decide what his path of action would be.

"Nick, how can I help you, son?" Brooks' amiable tone interrupted Nick's thoughts. Nick pushed the conflict from his mind and focused his attention back to the detective. He shuffled some papers to the side of the desk before locking his sharp gaze on Nick. Nick cleared his throat. "Ah, Sir. I understand the protocols around divulging information to junior officers such as myself, however, I'm increasingly concerned about this stalker who, upon being released, broke his bail conditions and went back to The Valley. Can you tell me who or what he is looking for there? As you know, this case affects me. If there is anything you can tell me, I would appreciate it. Sir."

An expectant silence settled over the office and Nick battled to keep eye contact with the senior officer. Detective Brooks linked his hands together over his desk and sighed. "He will be questioned shortly, and we will be getting to the bottom of this. If you, or your colleagues, are in anyway a target, you will be notified."

Nothing more could be offered. Nick knew this. He would have to wait. "Is he getting locked up? Or released with the same conditions?"

"Considering circumstances surrounding this case, we are going to hold him until a court hearing."

Relief coursed through Nick's body, knowing that the detective understood his predicament and that the guy was going to be in custody for a while. He gave a nod and stood. "Thank you, sir."

Mind clear, Nick left the detective's office and headed back to his desk, pausing only to check the noticeboard. A grin lit his features when he saw that Eddie was rostered on the same shifts as he was this week.

That guy was great value – that would help take his mind off things.

Renting a place with him would be good fun.

Nick mulled over the notices of new persons of interest, missing persons, lost dogs, and general housekeeping on the noticeboard, while thoughts of moving in with Eddie teased the corners of his mind.

He'd done his budget. He could afford it, and in the long term it wouldn't put him back too far in saving for a deposit.

Yeah. He'd do it.

This year was going to end with a bang.

CHAPTER TWELVE

"*G*o, go, go!"
"Hurry!"
"Just roll it already. Roll it!"

Nick leaned against the bricks of the hall and watched the icebreaker Dave had picked. The youths were sitting in a large circle, while a table full of dress-up items and a block of chocolate sat in the middle. To get the chocolate, someone had to roll a giant foam die, get a six, run to the table, and put on all the dress-up items. Only then could they cut off a piece of chocolate using a fork and a butter knife – all before the next person who rolled a six could take over.

A belly laugh threatened to break Nick's stoic expression as he watched the game unfold. He crossed his arms as he watched Lexi and Hope bent over in laughter. No sooner had someone started putting the dress-up items on, then the next person was running to the middle for their turn at the chocolate. One youth,

Ben, had just got a piece of chocolate cut off when another youth, James, rolled a six and sprinted towards Ben. With force, James began pulling the dress-up items off Ben while he was still trying to get the cut piece of chocolate into his mouth.

"You joining in?" Dylan's raised voice sounded next to him, and Nick repositioned himself to be able to talk to Dylan above the noise. "Nah. Lexi and Hope can represent. Too tired from the morning shift."

"I reckon I'll have a go. That chocolate looks pretty tempting."

"Go to the supermarket, then!" Nick called after Dylan as he jogged towards the game. Watching as Dylan squeezed himself in between some youths, Nick sighed heavily as he glanced towards the youth café and locked eyes with Trent setting up the chairs. The man gave a good-natured flick of his wrist towards the game in progress as he mouthed "*Go.*"

A lopsided grin tipped Nick's mouth as he looked back at the icebreaker. He pushed himself off the wall and, hearing his name called, strode over to join in.

The game was moving fast. It wasn't long after Nick moved himself into the circle that the die was in his hands and a desire to win pumped through his veins. With more pizzazz than was necessary, Nick flipped the die and a six turned up. Slapped on his back from both sides, Nick sprinted like a horse towards the youth madly trying to cut a piece of chocolate off the block. Nick pulled the beanie off the young man's head before he knew what was happening, then in a haze of scrambling hands Nick found himself dressed up head to toe and holding the cutlery in a pair of glove-covered hands. The noise of the room had faded to white noise as he tried to cut the chocolate block; his focus square on the chocolate shavings that were coming off under the pressure he was putting on the blunt butter knife.

A shout broke into his concentration and, without looking, his mind registered someone must have rolled a six. Any moment he'd be tackled by the next player as they tried to get their hands on a piece of the chocolate. He thrust the knife harder, faster. A taste of the chocolate was all he wanted. Suddenly he was knocked off-balance. Sprawled on his side, Nick turned his attention to who was trying to take the slippers off his feet. Dylan had one slipper off when Nick tucked the other foot under himself and scrambled back to continue cutting the chocolate. The scarf around his neck slipped off at the same time the beanie was yanked off his head. In his peripheral, Nick could see the youths ignoring their own turns and cheering himself or Dylan on in the scrimmage. Almost through cutting the chocolate, Nick was focusing hard when Dylan's hand grasped the hand holding the knife. Nick felt it slip out of his thick, gloved hand.

Unable to hold in his laughter, Nick clenched his fist to keep the glove on while Dylan tried to pull it off. All of a sudden, a whistle blew.

Once.

Twice.

Three times.

Dylan's grip loosened and Nick turned to the direction of the whistle as the noise in the hall subsided like the receding rumble of thunder.

Dave stood on the stage, a fatherly smile across his features and the whistle poised at his mouth. "How many of you wanted that chocolate?" Dave's voice rang out over the hall. Nick looked around the eager faces of the young people as they all raised their hands, sharing chuckles with each other.

Dave gave a knowing nod. "How many of you ran so hard at the person in front of you? You pulled off the dress-up items with gusto and put some real muscle into sawing off a chunk off that melt-in-your-mouth, smooth, Belgian milk chocolate?"

Groans rose up from the youths at Dave's description of the chocolate. Nick found himself swallowing at the thought of it, too. He had almost eaten that piece he was working on before Dylan tackled him. He glanced at Dylan. The man was side-eyeing him and Nick shouldered him before turning his attention back to Dave. Dave's expression had turned serious, here came the message. Nick crossed his arms and swept his gaze over the youths. They must have sensed the turn in topic because they looked to be in frozen animation with unblinking and still, eyes glued to their youth minister.

"Guys." Dave said, his tone somber. "How many of you are living your walk with Jesus with that much enthusiasm?" Dave pointed to the chocolate table. "You jumped through so many hurdles, no matter how difficult or impossible to even get a piece of chocolate – because you wanted it. You threw yourselves into it. The chocolate in this game of life is your eternity. How serious are you going to be over it? The Bible says the return of Jesus will be like a thief in the night. When He comes back, it's game over for each of us. So, let's get serious, yes?"

Nick scratched a non-itch behind his ear as he watched Dave's message hit the mark with a number of the youth. A vague disquiet stirred within him. That youth in the accident that he kept dreaming about, his six had come up, his game ended, and he was gone. Had he known Jesus?

"Frightening to consider, isn't it?"

Nick drew his spiraling thoughts in and looked at Trent. He was watching the youths with that imperceptible look of his, that same look that he was no doubt looking at Nick with just moments before. "What is?"

Trent peered back at him. "The fact that any moment could be our last. That we are only here because of the life sustained in us by Jesus Christ, who wakes us up every morning and protects us during each day. But it's more frightening to consider, what if our number comes up and we don't know Jesus? Isn't it? To not have that hope of life after death."

An uncomfortable heat traveled up the back of Nick's neck as he looked back at his friend. His heart began to thump. "I can't get past it. That night of the accident. It's never far from my mind. I..." Nick swallowed what felt like a tennis ball. "Trent, why did you come over that night?"

A bump on his side snapped Nick's attention back to the present like he was coming out of a dream. Hope stood next to him, buzzing like a fully charged battery. "What are we talking about here?"

Mind sluggish, Nick was trying to reorient himself in the room when Lexi and Dylan them. Lexi's face held a rosy flush, and her hands were on her hips as she looked to be catching her breath. "Are you guys joining in the games?"

Nick looked beyond Lexi and Hope to see the youths engaged in a high energy running race. It looked like several of them were holding hands and chasing after the others who were fleeing before them like mice from a sinking ship. "We were just debriefing Dave's message." He covered.

"Oh, before I forget," Lexi gave a click of her fingers and pointed to Nick, her expression turning serious. "How'd you go with, ah, your work stuff?"

A moment passed until Nick recalled what Lexi was asking him about. "He's locked up until a hearing."

"So, we can all relax." Trent added, and Nick bobbed his head in agreement. He was still trying to move past what was drawn out of him by the conversation with Trent just moments ago. He felt Trent had skirted the issue he was battling with, or had he nailed it? He wasn't sure – he needed time to think. "Oh Dylan, we'd better get over to the café. The kids are beating us to the food." Lexi said to Dylan, her focus back on the café. As Dylan and Lexi moved away, Nick glanced at Hope. She was staring in Trent's direction. "You knew what was going on with that guy, didn't you? I mean, of course you knew."

Trent's eyes fell upon Hope, but whatever response he had, he kept it to himself.

A prickling sensation began to tickle the back of Nick's neck as he watched the exchange between the two.

It was too familiar. He thought Hope was with Josh, so what was going on there?

His mind whirred. As soon as youth was over for the night, he'd take Hope aside and ask.

CHAPTER THIRTEEN

*D*ylan's Harley rumbled outside the hall as Nick went about last checks before closing up for the night. In the post-youth-night silence, his ears rang ever so slightly in the wake of the noise that had been there not half an hour ago.

Once everything was put away, he jumped down from the stage and strode the length of the hall towards the kitchen to check on how Hope going. He knew Trent and Dave were talking in Dave's office, so if he could grab a few moments alone with Hope he could get to the bottom of what was going on between her and Trent.

The swing door gave easily under his palm and, as he entered the kitchen, Hope's head popped up from behind the island bench. "Hey!" Hope greeted him before lowering her eyes again. "I'm just putting the mugs away, then I'll be good to go. You done out there?"

"Yeah, I'm done." Nick leaned back against the bench and listened to the soft clunk of each mug being put back in place, then watched Hope as she got back to her feet and took another look around the kitchen. "I reckon we're finished. The kitchen looks just like we found it."

Hope gave a nod of her head as if satisfied with her work before she moved around the island bench to leave. "Ok, let's get going. Are Dave and Trent gone already?"

Nick held up a hand. "Just give us a sec, please Hope. I wanna ask you something."

A surprised look flashed across Hope's face and she halted. Lassoing her bag strap around her shoulder she flashed a smile. "Fire away. What's up?"

"What's the deal with you and Trent?"

The residual ringing in Nick's ears continued as a silence fell over the room. Keeping his gaze set on her, he watched a number of expressions cross her features as she toyed with her bag strap. A blush began to spread across her cheeks. Her mouth worked as though she was looking to find the right words to answer his question, though nothing was coming out. Nick cleared his throat. "You two got a thing going on?"

"No!" Hope recoiled and Nick noticed her hand grip the strap of her bag. "No, Nick! I'm with Josh."

Nick gave a cool nod of his head as he crossed his arms. "Ok, then what has been going on between you two this last month?"

It was distracting how uncomfortable she looked, and Nick found his interest heightening the longer she took to answer the question. He decided to prompt her. "Has he done something that hurt you?"

"No."

"Upset you?"

"No."

"Same questions; someone else?"

"No. Nick." Hope's voice was hushed as she unhooked her bag strap from around her shoulder and placed it on the island bench. "Quite the opposite really."

"Well, out with it, Meyer. Whatever it is, it can't be that hard to tell me." Nick could hear his voice beginning to sound edgy, and that was not the right way to get someone to talk. He pushed off the bench and stood before, palms outstretched. "C'mon. It's just me. Get it off your chest – whatever it is."

Hope took her eyes off her bag and looked at him. He watched her eyes search his and he knew she was debating whether to tell him the truth or not. He gave a slow dip of his head to encourage her. Hope sighed, then straightened and held her hands up to him as if she was expecting him to get angry at her from what she was about to say.

"You remember that 'come as a Bible character' dress up night we had a couple of months ago?"

Nick gave a sardonic smile. "Yes. Why?"

"Well, I don't think that Trent's costume that night… was a… costume."

The nervous expression and fingernail Hope was now chewing on halted him in his instant dismissal of what she had said. He raised an eyebrow, keeping the laugh he felt at bay. "Let me get this straight – you think Trent's an angel?"

It was like Hope hadn't heard her own thoughts said back to her. She rolled her eyes and gave a wave of her hand. "Don't think that for a second I haven't had this conversation with myself many times. I know how ridiculous it sounds."

The smile Nick was trying to repress began to show and Hope gave him a frustrated shove. "Oh, go home. Forget I said anything."

"I can't, and I won't."

Hope grabbed her bag and made for the door. Nick hooked her elbow and turned her back to him. "Ok. Ok. I'll be serious. Tell me why you think this."

There was a reluctancy about Hope, though the tension in her arm relaxed so Nick let go, trusting she had decided to stay. Hope rejoined him at the island bench and put her bag back down. "Ok. But if you laugh once, I'm out of here."

Nick grinned, though gave her a nod. "Why did you start thinking this? It's pretty far out there."

'Oh, I know!" Hope gave a vigorous nod of her head. "I started to wonder when I realized he knew things that I hadn't told you guys. Like that disastrous party bus I went on. He knew about it and warned me not to go. Oh, and you know the night of Shaun and Renee's engagement, when Renee took off and then Shaun disappeared?"

Nick gave a nod of his head. Regardless of what he was thinking, Hope was convinced of what she believed. He'd hear her out.

"What nobody knows is that Shaun and I bumped into each other on the beach that night. I thought Josh and I were over, he thought he and Renee were over, and..."

Nick felt his stomach bottom out. "Tell me you guys didn't..."

Hope grabbed his arm. Her eyes wide and urgent. "We didn't. But it was close. My phone rang and when I looked at it there was no caller I.D. But I took that interruption as an escape and got outta there... only to run into Trent on Main Street. Phone. In. Hand. Coincidence?"

Nick gave a slight shake of his head, relief flooded his body knowing that Hope hadn't crossed the line with Lexi's older brother, Shaun. He gestured for her to continue.

"So that night was also the night that Jack ended up in hospital. I was talking to Trent, when I remember he started looking all edgy, told me to go home, and then just took off. And who was at the hospital first?"

Nick felt his curiosity ignite. "Trent."

"Go back further," Hope continued. "The car accident you were a first responder to. Who just happened to stop by your home when you arrived back after your shift, and messaged us all to pray for you?"

Nick closed his eyes as images of what he'd seen that night flashed through his mind. "Trent."

"Remember that afternoon when Dylan was out playing footy and Jack attacked their mum? Dylan's mum said something disturbed Jack and he ran from the house, remember? One guess who that was. She doesn't recall anyone around the house, though. It's like that night Brad's roommate just happened to come home, because his date stood him up, just in time before Brad could hurt Lexi? Oh, and remember the night when Dylan laid into Brad? Who pulled him off before he could do too much damage to Brad?"

Nick held up a hand. "Ok, Ok, Hope. There's a lot you're putting on Trent's shoulders there. Some of it is just supposition, the rest could very well be coincidences."

"They're not coincidences, Nick." Hope pressed.

The firmness in her voice and the intensity shining back at him through her eyes sent a small shiver down his spine. "Fine. Let's play this out then. Say this is all Trent. Why us, why here?"

"Is it so hard to believe an angel is working with a church? More specifically, with a group of youth leaders?"

Conscious of the time and that Dave and Trent would be wrapping up their meeting soon, Nick ran a hand over his hair, keen to move the conversation on. "No, it's not hard to believe. But as I said, why us? What's he waiting for?"

Hope shrugged and waved her hands over her head. "Oh I don't know, Nick. I've only just put the pieces together. But, from what I know and seen, angels protect."

Nick took a quick glance at the clock on the wall. It was almost 10 p.m. They needed to finish up and get home. "So, you think he's protecting us?"

"It's a theory. Yes."

"From? Please explain this theory to me."

Hope's mouth pressed into a thin line as she looked back at him. He wasn't going to feed into her theory by offering anything. What she had said had planted a seed in him, but he still needed more information and time to think it over. He made a rolling hand motion. "Go on."

A moment passed between them while Nick held Hope's stare, then with a sigh she glanced away.

"Look, Nick. I hate saying it, but I can't help thinking about Jack. Yes, I know he has been moved to a safe place, but these guys who Jack was dealing with obviously want their money. If they can't get it from Jack, who will they come for next?"

Nick pocketed his hands. He knew. Dylan had mentioned it too.

"Friends and family." Hope said with a poke in Nick's arm. "We... particularly you Nick because of your job... are potential targets. Therefore...Trent."

A sprinkle of goosebumps ran up Nick's arms. He knew she must have thought a lot about this and wouldn't have told him anything unless he had pressed her for information. He read her eyes – this was no fanciful thought inspired by some book she'd read or movie she'd watched. It was real. To her, for the moment, at least. He was going to have to do some thinking.

And watch Trent closer.

CHAPTER FOURTEEN

The church grounds were abuzz with innumerous conversations, and the air was filled with the scents of soups, baked breads, and the pungent aroma of blossom on the ornamental pear trees that dotted the churches fence line.

Nick placed his plate on the table and sat heavily into a chair, stretching his arms above his head as he let out a wide yawn.

"C'mon now, the service wasn't that long." Dylan drew a chair out next to Nick and, after putting his own plate down, sat next to him. "It's not like you to struggle to stay awake during church. What's going on?"

Nick gave an absentminded shake of his head. There was so much going on, it was hard to know where to start. It was also beginning to disturb his sleep. Not to mention the reoccurring dream that kept waking him up. "Just this guy who came back to the Plaza – it plays on my mind a bit."

"Mine too."

Dylan was now shoveling a hearty mouthful of rice salad into his mouth. He didn't sound too worried. Nick turned to check, "Lexi told you what happened?" Dylan gave a nod while he continued chewing. Nick turned to look over at the rest of the gathering, ran a hand through his hair and scratched the back of his head. "So, you knew Trent was there?"

"Yeah." Dylan shoveled another mouthful in. After taking another glance around, Nick leant forward. Clasping his hands and laying them on the table, Nick trained his gaze square on Dylan, wanting to catch the slightest flicker in his eyes. He wanted to gauge Dylan's reaction to his burning question. "Do you think it was strange that Trent was there?"

"Hey guys!" Hope's shrill voice interrupted the momentary connection Nick had with Dylan before he looked across the table to greet who had joined them. "Hope. Josh."

"Fellas." Josh greeted through a grin, before shouldering into Hope and sharing a soft chuckle with her. Nick couldn't help but smile at the two of them – they really were a well-suited couple. Hope was buzzing, appearing to be just in control of herself – on the edge of the seat, luminous smile, twitchy. Josh on the other hand, was holding something back. There was a subtle blush over his tanned face which heightened Nick's curiosity.

"Guys we have some exciting news!" Hope blurted out and Nick heard Dylan cough. Without looking at him, Nick gave Dylan a few raps on his back. Josh tilted his head towards Hope. "Can't you let me tell them, Hope?"

Laughter bubbled out of Hope just as Lexi and Trent joined the table. "What are we laughing at?" Lexi's voice rose over Josh's attempts to quell the elated Hope. Nick could not deny the heavy thuds within his chest at whatever was about to be revealed – surely it was not an engagement. He leaned back in his seat, eyeing both parties when Josh spoke through a broad grin. "Before Dylan here chokes on his rice salad, the news is, I have decided to get baptized!"

Hope emitted a restrained squeal as she turned to Josh, taking one of his hands in hers. Nick studied her – her smile was one he had never glimpsed before: pure joy. He smiled in response to the happiness emanating from her but couldn't help thinking about Alice. Would she ever come to faith like Josh had? And what would that mean for their relationship? He was so happy for Josh and Hope, but perhaps a little envious too? What if Alice and he were never on the same page? Nick was brought back into the moment when Dylan leant over the table, offering his hand to Josh. "That is fantastic news, brother." Josh clasped Dylan's hand firmly, before accepting the same gesture from Trent. Lexi had already jumped up and had rounded the table to give Josh an awkward side hug. Nick laughed and reached a hand across the table when Lexi released him. "What a testimony you have mate. When is the baptismal service?"

The smile Josh wore reached his eyes as he reached across the table to shake Nick's hand; the man was almost incandescent. Hope and he looked like a poster couple. "Thanks Nick." Josh beamed, "I have spoken to Pastor Walker about a Christmas service. It depends how I get through the studies first."

"Oh, you will be fine!" Hope jumped in. "You are with me, remember?" Her playful tone had a haughty edge to it which drew a chuckle from Nick, and he turned his attention back to the cooling plate of food before him.

Light-hearted conversation carried on, mingling with the sounds of laughter and the tinkle of cutlery. Lexi leaned her elbows on the picnic table and eagerly requested Hope tell them about her recent mission trip.

As Hope recounted all the details of the mission trip, even describing a story of what could only have been an obvious miracle, Nick's attention drifted. An elbow to his side brought his attention to Dylan. He whispered, not disturbing the conversations going on around the table, "so big day for you tomorrow brother, are you all set to move in with your workmate?"

Nick readjusted himself on the seat while drawing in a deep breath. "Yeah. Everything is boxed up ready to go."

"That's come up quick." Dylan replied. "How are you feeling about it?"

"It's going to be different. My folks are on the fence about it, but I'm really looking forward to it."

"Need a hand with anything?" Dylan asked before taking a bite of a piece of bread.

Nick gave a shake of his head. "Nah. Got a trailer sorted. Thanks for the offer, though."

With a good-natured slap to his shoulder, Dylan went back to his meal and Nick tuned back into another story Hope was sharing. Though he listened, he couldn't ignore the excitement that was tickling his nerves about tomorrow.

Tomorrow was not only the start of a new week, but it was also the start of a new chapter for him.

CHAPTER FIFTEEN

*I*t was still a surreal thought to Nick, that he was heading down an impromptu path moving in with a work colleague – one that he couldn't say he knew all that well.

The house Eddie was renting was in an older suburb of the city, only about twenty minutes from The Valley, so Nick could still attend youth nights and church. And it was also twenty minutes from their station. There was a very simple stone garden in the front, which meant outdoor maintenance would be low, and the orange and apple trees in the back yard would give him his favorite fresh fruits whenever he desired.

The solid wood door swung open before he reached the porch and he laughed seeing Eddie standing in the doorway with a beaming smile and a beer in hand. "Welcome home, son."

With a chuckle, Nick readjusted the bag over his shoulder, then stepped over the threshold into his new digs.

The narrow hallway went past a theatre room and Eddie's large unkempt bedroom. Further on, it opened out into a large kitchen and living area with a doorway that led to his bedroom, the bathroom, and the laundry. Dumping his bag on the kitchen bench he turned to Eddie.

Eddie lifted his drink in a toast and nodded. To the new beginning. He chugged back the rest of the beer then ran the back of his hand over his mouth and placed the empty bottle on the kitchen bench. "You want one?"

Nick shook his head. "Nah. Don't touch the stuff."

"Ok then," Eddie said with a clap of his hands that echoed throughout the open living area. "Let's get you moved in."

Two hours later, Nick flopped into Eddie's oversized sofa and draped his arms over the back. His bedroom was set up, bed made, pictures hung… this was home now. It felt odd but thrilling at the same time.

"Knock. Knock."

Hearing Alice's voice float down the hallway, Nick sat up from his seat and jogged out towards her. "I wasn't expecting to see you today."

He loved the way she dropped her chin and looked up at him as he approached, and he wasted no time in scooping her up in a hug. To feel her arms around him brought an instant calm to his mind after the whirlwind that the day had been. He took a long deep breath of the scent of her hair before putting her back on her feet. She was beaming at him. "What is it?" Nick grinned back at her.

"Hey Alice." Eddie said, brushing past them with a box held above his head. "Hey." Alice called after him, not taking her eyes off Nick. "I brought you a little something."

Nick watched as Alice disappeared back out the front door. He took a step to go after her, but she reappeared, her hands behind her back. A wide grin broke out over Nick's face as she approached him. Stopping just in front of him, she drew a Bonsai tree from behind her back. "Happy moving in day!"

"Wow. A Bonsai." Nick raised an eyebrow as he looked from the tall, elegant tree nestled in its elaborate ceramic pot, back to his girlfriend's face – unsure what to make of the gift.

"It's a cedar Bonsai." Alice's voice was hushed in reverence as she held it out for him to take. "It symbolizes protection and strength."

"So, me... as a tree?" Nick offered, knowing his impish joke would annoy her. He chuckled when she looked away with a disgusted look on her face. When she turned back to him, he bent and gave her a kiss as he took the gift. "Just playing." Nick said, his voice low. "I think it's great. Where should I put it?"

The smile came back to Alice's face, and she slipped past him into the house. He turned and followed her down the hall, eyeing the miniature cedar tree cradled in his hands. He was stuck on why she picked something with a focus on protection.

"I think it should go here." Alice's voice was chirpy and Nick looked up to see where she was. She had her arms open towards the kitchen bench like she was waiting for a performer to enter who she had just introduced. "The Bonsai needs indirect light for around six hours a day. This spot on your bench should be perfect!"

The ceramic pot clinked on the bench as Nick slid it to where Alice suggested. The tree was magnificent, and he found himself moved by the thought she had put into selecting such a significant gift. Turning to her, he took her hands in his. "Thank you. I do really like it."

A soft smile lit her features before she moved into his arms and lifted her chin up to him. He'd just felt the honeyed brush of her lips against his when an exaggerated throat clearing across the other side of the room, interrupted their moment. With a glacial pace, Nick turned to look at where his house mate was standing and raised an eyebrow. Eddie held his phone up as if he'd interrupted nothing. "Pizza?"

"Sure." Nick said, growl in warning with the word. Eddie played back with a salute before heading down the hallway towards his room. "Nice Bonsai, by the way."

Nick dropped his head and chuckled before looking back at Alice. "You staying for dinner?"

"I'd love to." She answered before resuming their moment. Then, drawing back slightly, she gushed at him. "I'm so happy you like the gift. I wanted to get something that had meaning and would last a long time. And I know what a big move this is for you. I want you to know I support you all the way."

Nick gazed back at her. Her hair looked like rippling satin in the sunlight streaming through the window behind her. Her eyes sparkled back at him, and that cheeky grin could almost cause him to lose his train of thought.

Almost.

"Let me ask you something." Nick leant back against the bench, holding Alice's hands loosely. "Why a Bonsai with protection significance? I'd have thought one with new beginnings, happiness or prosperity meanings might have been a more standard choice."

Alice toyed with his fingers. "I saw that one and felt it was the right one. You know, everyone can use a bit of protection over them…"

"And you think a tree gives me that?"

"Giving the cedar tree is symbolic of me wishing that over you."

"Ah, I see." Nick murmured, trying to keep his mind on the conversation rather than the way his stunning girlfriend purred her words while closing the gap between them. "Do you think wishes are more powerful than prayers?"

The shuttering of her eyes was subtle, and the parting of her lips was not an invitation. Nick kept his expression neutral as he waited for whatever she would say next. He knew she didn't like it when he steered conversations to matters of beliefs – a factor in their relationship that sat like a weight on his mind. Would it eventually be the deal-breaker between them?

Alice sighed. "I think whatever works for each individual or brings them comfort in hard times. That's what matters." Her eyes moved to where he'd placed the Bonsai. "This means something to me, and I feel better knowing it's with you. I guess like when you pray for someone."

Nick considered Alice's perspective. He knew she had no background in faith, but rather a concept that we are all connected and are here to help each other. To her, there was significance to her picking this gift for him. "Yeah, I can agree with that. Ok, so what makes you feel I need this? Do you think I need protecting?"

"Pizza's here in ten." Eddie's voice sounded from the front of the house. Alice's contemplative expression gave way to a gentle smile. "Thanks!" She called over Nick's shoulder.

"Yeah, thanks." Nick echoed, not taking his eyes off Alice. "You were saying?"

"Well, yeah. I guess I do." Alice lifted her shoulder; a cute thing he noticed she did when a little unsure of herself. "Call it women's intuition."

A lopsided grin tipped the corner of Nick's mouth as he gazed back at her. "Women's intuition, eh? I think that's what I would call, the Holy Spirit talking to you."

CHAPTER SIXTEEN

Nick lay on his bed, arms behind his head, listening an owl outside his window. Its haunting calls soothed the traffic jam of thoughts that were keeping him awake.

Over and over, he recalled things Hope had said. Events from the past, the trouble Jack was in, the eerie fact that Alice felt he needed protection… was it all coincidence? A large part of his mind argued that it was just that, but the part currently keeping him awake wondered – what if it wasn't? As much as he wanted to disagree with what Hope had said about Trent, he realized he couldn't dispute it.

So, what did that mean for him? How could he relate to Trent, one of his best friends, from now on?

With a growl, Nick rolled over and fumbled for his phone. 2:08a.m.

He had to get some sleep. He would see Trent at the leadership meeting tonight, and if his instinct told him to keep silent, he would. But if it told him to go after him, he would.

*   *   *   *

Nick flicked on the lights and sirens as Geoff dropped down a gear and their patrol car rocketed forwards. Nick scanned the highway ahead, anticipating what they were enroute to assist with. An overhead chopper caught his attention – air ambulance. He exchanged a glance with Geoff. Sometimes, no words were needed.

Déjà vu transported his mind back to the night that haunted him, and his palms became clammy. He rubbed his hands over his thighs, wishing his heart rate would slow.

"You ok, Nick?"

Nick nodded. "Yes, sir. ETA ten minutes."

"I need you to focus." Geoff wove the car through the traffic on the highway, while Nick held the grab handle beside him in a death grip. Keeping his mind on Jesus rather than the speed Geoff was going, Nick remembered the Lord's promise and prayed for the spirit of fear to leave him and a sound mind to settle in its place.

The crash site appeared on the horizon and Nick felt Geoff shifting through the gears as they approached. His jaw clenched. *God be with me.*

Thankful his role was to divert traffic around the four-car pileup, Nick went about placing traffic cones and flashing hazard signs along the highway to ensure nobody else was injured. The cries and groans of the injured carried over the road noises and the firm, controlled voices of the ambulance crew as they worked on each patient. He could see other police officers setting up barriers and interviewing witnesses to determine who was responsible. Almost one year on the force and not one day had been the same. While he liked the variety, these accidents were getting harder for him to endure.

Waving traffic around the cones, Nick reigned in the panic trying to steal his focus, and he concentrated only on what was happening around him in that moment.

The air ambulance soon left, followed by the paramedics; lights and sirens wailing. It was time for the cleanup and then they'd be headed back to the station.

His work cell phone rang, and he clicked answer on the wireless headset he wore. "Marshall."

"Nick, it's Lexi. Sorry to ring you at work, but I need to talk to you."

Nick frowned as he continued waving traffic by. She sounded breathless. Worried. "Ok, go on."

There was a shuddering sound as she exhaled. "I've just got home from work and checked the mail as I usually do. Nick… there was a note in the mailbox."

The hairs on the back of Nick's neck rose.

"They know where I live now. What do I do?"

A semitrailer rumbled past. Nick waited until the noise had subsided. "Take it down to The Valley Headquarters immediately, they'll tell you what to do next. I'll inform my supervisors. You should touch base with the others, and I'll catch up with you all tonight at Dave's."

Another shuddering breath cut short by the sound of Lexi's Jeep starting up.

"Lexi, you'll be ok. I've gotta run."

"Ok. See you tonight. Bye."

Nick glanced over to where Geoff was working. The accident site was still crawling with cleanup crew members. It looked like he would be here a while, and then he had the rest of his shift to finish so there would be no chance of leaving early. He dialed Detective Brooks' number.

This was not good.

CHAPTER SEVENTEEN

*N*ick yawned as he made his way towards the door of his youth minister's home.

The day had been one incident after another. No sooner had he and Geoff pulled away from the accident site, then they were called to a domestic disturbance where he was spat on. Then they were called to a retirement village for a welfare check and finally, just a block from their station, Geoff recognized a vehicle that had been reported as stolen – which led to a high-speed chase. As he had followed Geoff into the station with their handcuffed perp, while ignoring the vile language coming out of his mouth, Nick had ached for a cuppa and a hot shower. Though, not willing to be late to Leadership, Nick had skipped the shower and was looking forward to enjoying a cuppa at the leadership meeting.

Laughter flowed out from Dave's library windows and mixed with the happy chirping of birds in Linda's garden. At least the mood inside was jovial. Not what he was expecting after the phone call from Lexi. All afternoon he'd been anxious to talk to his friends. Detective Brooks had taken the threat as seriously as Nick had imagined it was, and hung up from him within seconds. He'd not heard anything since.

Nick made his way through to the library. An odd mix of adrenaline and weariness battled for supremacy within his body.

"Good evening, Nick." Dave waved him in and gestured to the pew by the window. "Great to see you all. Before we start, Trent is unable to join us this evening. He says he has some personal business to take care of."

Nick fired a look at Hope. Her eyes found his briefly before she looked back at Dave. Yep, she was thinking the same. Nick sipped his drink and wondered what personal business Trent had. Then the thought flashed through his mind of the story Hope had told him about Trent taking off one night when they were talking.

Jack had ended up in hospital that night.

A chill ran up Nick's spine and he readjusted himself on the pew. Something was brewing.

"Nick?"

Nick looked up at Dave. "Dave?"

"We were just talking about what everyone's plans are for next year, as the end of this year will be upon us before we know it. Are you planning on staying with the leadership team? How are you doing with the travel and working the eighty-hour fortnights?"

"Yeah, put me down again. It's been a bit of an adjustment, but I'm doing well. Thanks."

"Great. That's all of you back for next year. Trent confirmed with me earlier today, and Josh is keen to remain as a backup if any of you are unavailable. Now, with that sorted, let's dive into the plan for this weekend. This Sabbath is Josh's baptism, so I feel a very practical icebreaker is needed." Dave handed some papers over the desk to Lexi, and she began to pass them around.

He continued. "It's a messy one, but they'll love it, and the message will stay with them."

"Dave," Lexi put a hand up, her eyes on the paper in her hands. "The parents might not like the request for white T-shirts to be worn."

"Everything we use will be completely water-based. Nothing to worry about. And there's a note in there about making sure they wear their swimsuits underneath. But it's important we all start the night in white to drive home the final message."

"I like this concept." Dylan folded the paper and tucked it into his jeans. "Ok, some parents might grumble, but I think that when they understand the message, they'll come around."

"And it's not like we do this all the time." Nick added.

Dave clapped his hands. "Great. Linda and I are going to organize a towel for each youth to take home with the text 'Acts 22:16' embroidered on it. The rest of you, what you're to bring is listed on your sheet. I have emailed Trent a copy as well, so he will be up-to-speed."

There was the sound of whisper-thin paper flipping, and Nick looked to where the girls sat. Hope had her Bible out. Delight crossed her features as her finger trailed the open page before her. "Nice one, Dave. The verse says this guys: 'And now what are you waiting for? Get up, be baptized and wash your sins away, calling on His name.' It's perfect."

While Nick listened to the room discuss details of the upcoming youth night, a growing awareness of the day's issues began to creep back into his conscious thought. He scanned the room, scrutinizing the expressions on his friends' faces. He saw it then – strain behind their smiles, an odd pitch to the laughter, and fidgeting in their seats.

The same thing was on their minds too. As soon as the meeting was over, they needed to debrief with each other.

* * * *

"Shall we catch up at the beach?" Dylan's voice was hushed as they left Dave's home and moved towards their cars. "Or do we just spill what's on our minds here and now?"

Nick pocketed his hands as his eyes swept the area outside Dave's. It was private and safe. It would do for now. Frowning, Nick cleared his throat and looked at Lexi. "How'd you go this afternoon?"

Lexi brushed her fringe aside. "They're going to put surveillance around our home, and we've been advised to change our security systems. Dad was making phone calls as I headed out to come here."

Nick looked at Dylan. "How's things at your place?"

"We had a visit from the detective leading the investigation. They're not happy that it's just mum and me at the house. So, Lachlan's pretty much moved in with us now – he's staying in Jack's room." Dylan chuckled as he added the last bit and Nick grinned. It was good to see Dylan's mum finding someone again, but if they got married there's be no need for the separate rooms.

"Does this mean the police are getting serious about this guy?" Hope leaned in and her voice was lowered as if eavesdroppers were near. Nick nodded gravely; his mouth pressed into a thin line. "I'm afraid so. They'll be trying to flush Jack out. Detective Brooks assures me they are close to catching these guys. They're close. In the meantime, guys, be careful."

Lexi shivered and stepped closer to Dylan and his arm came around her. "What about you, Nick? Do you think you're at risk?"

"I did wonder about that," Nick replied, "but I'm assured by Detective Brooks that Dylan and his family are the immediate targets. I'm not even on their radar. I'll be ok."

CHAPTER EIGHTEEN

*N*ick connected the garden hose to his portable shower pump system and went to turn it on. The whole week was meant to swelter with the mercury predicted to nudge 40 degrees by Friday.

Friday.

Nick grinned to himself. They couldn't have asked for better weather for what they had planned.

The splutter and hiss as the hose came to life added a peaceful element to the late morning quiet. Suddenly a hammering, base sound which grew in intensity, sent the birds erupting from the trees.

Eddie's silver MX6 came into view and turned into the drive. A minute later, silence settled once again over the neighborhood and Eddie stepped out of his car.

"Any idea what that doof-doof music is doing to your brain there, mate?" Nick moved back to the portable shower. Eddie took off his sunglasses and hooked them in his shirt as he approached, his eyes square on the portable shower. "I'm sure you're going to tell me."

A smirk lifted the corner of Nick's mouth. "I'd love to, but your alpha brain wouldn't grasp anything explained to you at the moment."

Eddie turned to him with a bored expression before thumbing a gesture to the shower. "What are you doing here? Going camping for the weekend?"

Nick gave a shake of his head as he tested the hot and cold taps of the shower. "It's for youth night, mate. We're gonna get the kids all messy and they'll need to clean up afterwards. So, I'm just making sure she's running right."

A lightness crept into Eddie's features as he folded his arms and tilted his head to the side. "Go on, then. Tell me what you lot are up to this coming youth night?"

"Because there is a baptism service this Saturday, we are just laying out a practical activity about why baptism is needed for Friday night youth." Nick grinned, knowing his answer didn't really answer the question. Eddie raised an eyebrow in response. "Baptism?"

Turning the shower taps off, Nick focused his attention on his housemate. "Ok, look at it like a marriage ceremony. The believer in Jesus decides to make a public statement that they have given their life to Jesus, then they are immersed in water – which is a symbol of being cleansed of worldly dirt. Then they are raised up out of the water, ready to start a new life following Jesus."

Eddie gave a slow nod while his eyes scanned their front lawn in thought, then he looked back at Nick. "Have you been dunked?"

"I was baptized not long after graduating high school." Judging by the curiousness he sensed in Eddie, Nick ventured further. "Would you like to come to church this Sabbath and see the service?"

"Is Alice going?"

A frown furrowed Nick's forehead for a moment as he looked back at Eddie. "Nah, she's not big on coming to church."

Eddie began to move towards the house again, giving Nick a clap on the shoulder as he passed. "When you get her there, then ask me again."

With a resigned shake of his head, Nick watched his housemate make his way inside. The sound of the front door closing had a sense of finality about it. The discouragement he carried about Alice not coming to church was deepening, and Eddie's brush dismissal of the invitation didn't help.

The sun was beginning to beat down upon Nick so he decided to pack up. Crossing the lawn to turn off the garden hose, Nick let his mind wander. Josh was being baptized this Sabbath! That was a huge step in what seemed like just a short time. Nick had been with Alice for longer than Hope had been with Josh, and yet he couldn't get her to step foot inside his church.

Despondency lapped at his mind. Perhaps the Holy Spirit had been working on Josh for longer and Hope had come into the play at the eleventh hour, whereas he was in the early days of Alice's journey. "Do not give up hope," Nick murmured to himself as he packed up the shower. "God is outside of time and doesn't want anyone to be lost. As long as we work with Him, all things will come together in His time."

Exhausted from the heat, Nick made his way back inside. Thankful he didn't have to work today or tomorrow, he stepped into the cool of the house and joined Eddie in the living room. He was scrolling his Netflix account.

"Movie marathon afternoon?" Eddie took a few gulps from the beer can in his hand. Nick gave a nod. "I'm not going back out there again."

"Heads, Marvel. Tails, Pirates of the Caribbean." Eddie tossed a coin at Nick. Nick caught it while he took in Eddie's unblinking stare that was still focused on the 75inch TV before them. He flipped the coin.

"How's that alpha brain going?"

CHAPTER NINETEEN

*N*ick pulled off his sunglasses, placed them on the dash of his car, and stepped out into the muggy, late-afternoon air.

Laughter echoed over the empty expanse of lawn and Nick grinned. The night felt good already, he sensed a special blessing lay upon this night. "Dear God," Nick murmured, "please let this message sink in deep with the young people."

Moving to the rear of his car Nick took out the portable shower equipment then made his way towards the freshly mowed lawn of the church.

"Hey, Nick."

Nick straightened at Trent's voice calling nearby. Trent was stepping backwards out of the church's garden shed, dragging a large tarp along with him, still dressed as if he'd come from the work site. "Give us a hand with this tarp, can ya?"

With a few quick strides, Nick caught up with Trent and took the other side of the tarp. "Worked late this afternoon, eh?"

"Aw, we had to finish off the roof today as storms are forecast for tomorrow. I've got a change of clothes in the Ute though."

Nick fired a smirk at Trent. "Is it going to matter though?"

Trent chuckled and gave a quick shake of his head. "Not in the slightest!"

Working together they maneuvered the tarp into position on the lawn just as Hope pulled up, followed by Lexi in her Jeep. Then they positioned the camping shower not far from the tarp and while Trent jogged off to get changed, Nick hooked the shower up while listening to the rest of the team chat and set up around him.

At a sudden squeal, Nick was back on his feet and running over to the group. Had a spider or worse, a snake, appeared after rolling out the tarp on this muggy evening? Hope had Lexi by the shoulders and was jostling her playfully. "I'm just so excited. This night is going to be awesome!"

Lexi grabbed Hope's shoulders and played back the same way. "I know! And we all look smashing in our white T-shirts!"

"Then let's get set up," Dylan said with laughter in his voice, picking up a box and walking onto the mat. "They'll be arriving soon."

They were just laying out the last of the props when the first of the youths arrived for the evening. Nick stood back and looked over what they'd set up. Food dye of all colors, water-based paints, jelly cakes, pots of honey, crushed biscuits... he chuckled to himself. Looks of hesitancy and curiosity lit the youths' features, while hands and arms seem to subconsciously protect their white T-shirts.

The excitement Lexi and Hope had overflowed with earlier, now wove its way throughout Nick's body. He felt it dispel the stress that had been draining his energy, now he was every bit as keen to get into this icebreaker as the young people. Nick watched as Dave approach the ever-growing crowd from the church office, a large box tucked under his arm and wide grin on his face.

Nick knew what was in that box.

The youths were going to love this night.

"Welcome everyone." Dave called out, placing the box beside him on the lawn. "What a glorious evening it is, and what a mess it's going to become – for you."

Nick watched the youths' eyes travel over the items laid out on the tarp and exchange whispers with each other – their eyes large and mouths open in silent exclaim. Although they had no idea what was planned, they couldn't wait to get in amongst it. Just like it was in real life. With a derisive sniff, Nick gave a slight shake of his head and continued to listen to Dave's address.

"What we have here for you is free play! But on this warm evening, we've added an extra element. Anything on the tarp you can use to mess each other up with. One rule: you can't leave the mat to bring anything else into the play. Go."

In a blur, the youths raced towards the tarp, their laughter filled the air followed by squeals of both delight and shock as the first of the props went flying. Their white T-shirts were soon covered in blobs of purple, red, orange, blue, and yellow jelly; their hair matted with biscuits and honey. Some, while slipping over in the spilled food dyes, reached for the paint-filled sauce bottles and sent great arcs of paint over the play area covering unintended victims in the process.

Unable to resist, Nick tried his best combat glide towards a box of food dyes. Moving seamlessly amongst the youths, he was just within arm's reach of his goal when something struck him on the side of the head. Distracted, he turned to see who it was and found himself tackled to the tarp. Bodies piled up on his back and he felt himself pushed further into the mess smeared over the tarp. Laughter, loud and triumphant, sounded in his ear and he guessed there was at least four youths on his back holding him down.

One last reach for the box saw his fingertips just tip it towards him. Sauce bottles came rolling out and he grabbed two. Holding them back behind his head he squeezed them with all that he had.

A coughing and spluttering sounded and the weight upon his back lifted enough for him to roll out from underneath. Nick laughed as he watched them wiping color from their faces, while he struggled to regain his footing on the sodden tarp. All of a sudden, arms curled under his armpits and hoisted him to his feet.

"On your feet, Officer Marshall." Dylan's voice came from beside him. Nick turned to him, ready to pull him into the fray, when Dave's voice called everyone to order.

Hands on hips, Nick looked over the youths. "What a mess." He murmured to Dylan, who chuckled in reply as he ran the back of his hand across his forehead. "Wait until what happens next. Nothing like a practical application to a message." Dylan held out his fist and Nick bumped it in return, as the noise around them settled down.

"You've all had fun, I take it?" Dave called out. Heads bobbed and laughter was heard in response, while Dave moved towards the portable shower Nick had set up. Dave laid his hand on the frame of the shower, then gestured to everyone before him. "It is unavoidable. Living in this world means getting messy. I have a question for you all though; would any of you go to a fancy dinner looking the way you are?"

Nick looked around the gathered group once again and watched with interest as they looked over themselves, some clearly puzzled at the question. Many gave a shake of their heads while a couple scoffed and called out yes, drawing laughter from those around them. Unfazed, Dave continued.

"Jesus is coming back. He promised He will return to bring us to a very fancy dinner He is preparing for us in Heaven. And He asks us to be ready for it. But how? Well, in preparation for the baptismal service planned for Sabbath tomorrow, our activity is based on the one thing Jesus asks us to do: come to Him and let

Him make you clean. Step into the waters of baptism and wash the stinky, sticky, goopy, muck of the world off us and be ready for when He comes back."

Dave pressed a button to turn the shower on. "Each one of us will step into the shower and watch as the water washes all the mess off you. I ask that you watch all that is making you dirty slip away and run down the drain, leaving your white T-shirts white once again. No need for soap – everything we've used will wash off in water. Then, step out and grab a towel we've provided for you." Dave opened the box next to him and held a towel up. "Dry off, then then head back into the hall for café."

The mood had shifted. Nick knew the message had hit where it needed to. Many heads were bowed as if in thought and jokes had ceased. One by one, somewhat orderly for a group of teenagers, they made their way into the shower. When they stepped out the other side, Nick felt a warmth swell within his chest at their humbled expressions. They ran their hands over their wet but clean T-shirts, then looked up with a laugh or wondrous expression before Lexi and Hope wrapped them in towels and sent them off to the hall.

A hand fell upon Nick's shoulder, and he turned to see that Dylan and Trent had joined him. "Dave nailed it again."

Dylan gave a nod of his head. His gaze locked in the direction of the youths stepping in and out of the shower. "Yep. I think this will be one lesson that will stick with them."

"Remember, brothers," Trent spoke into the gentle evening breeze, "our job is to only sow the seed. Conviction is the work of the Holy Spirit."

CHAPTER TWENTY

*H*ands clasped loosely between his thighs, Nick turned to look at the sunlight streaming through the stained-glass windows and readjusted himself on the polished oak pew. He enjoyed baptismal services, just not the tiredness he felt creeping into his bones.

The worship team began playing and he turned his attention towards the front of the church, his eyes landing on Trent. There was a peace about the man as he played his acoustic guitar – as if he were the only person in the room. The hymn 'More Love to Thee' floated throughout the church, surrounding Nick like a warm embrace when he noticed Trent's gaze lock onto something behind him. Nick turned to see Hope and Josh enter.

An odd sensation stirred within him at the sight of them walking towards the front of the church together before taking a seat beside Pastor Walker, when a thought flashed into his mind: Alice wasn't ready yet.

He dropped his head, fixing his eyes on his hands. Hope had been blessed that her boyfriend had been converted and, while Nick was continually praying that Alice's heart would soften, this recent impression in his mind worried him.

"Are you ok?"

Nick looked over at Dylan, masking the worry he knew would be showing as lines across his forehead. He nodded. "Yeah. Just a bit overwhelmed with the strong floral smell going on in here."

Dylan chuckled. "I hear ya."

Lexi's head appeared from the other side of Dylan; she must have heard their exchange. "The hydrangeas and lavender are beautiful, guys." Her voice was hushed though held a sweet grace. "The deaconesses have done a great job."

Nick spoke around Dylan, keeping his tone light. "No one said it wasn't a nice display of flowers…"

"…It's just a bit much." Dylan added.

"Exactly." Nick settled back into his seat just as the Head Elder began the Divine Service.

Soon it was time for Pastor Walker's sermonette before calling Josh up to deliver his testimony.

Out of the corner of his eye, he noticed Hope sit forward; her chin resting on her fists as she leaned over her knees. Though she smiled, she looked nervous.

Nick looked back at Josh. He was impressed how Josh stood to his full 6-foot-3-inches height with squared shoulders, even though he'd never been a position to speak in front of the church before. Nick found himself drawn into the man's story – how he had been trying to work out who God was when, everywhere he looked, he only found hypocrites. He admired how Josh had kept asking, even though he said his questions caused his loved ones to be uncomfortable. Full of wonder, Nick smiled. He could see how God was using Josh long before Josh had figured out who God was. He looked at Hope, she had a tissue in her hand. God had even used Josh to help in her own journey with Him, well before Josh had believed...

A frown began to play upon Nick's forehead. Had he ever been used in God's hands like Josh had? He thought about Lexi and Dylan. Had they? While he knew it was not their business to know how God had used them, it would be encouraging at times to see the fruits of their labor.

An echo of Amen's sounded and Nick put his thoughts aside. Pastor Walker was moving toward Josh, then stood beside him with his hand on Josh's shoulder.

"Thank you for sharing your testimony, Josh. Such a powerful reminder to all of us to live what we believe, even if it means being different. Because people around us are searching for Jesus." Pastor Walker turned to Josh. "How has life been since you've given your life to Him?"

Josh let out a good-natured chuckle. "Like what I imagine a honeymoon to feel like. I've never known a family like the family of my now eternal brothers and sisters. I've never felt more welcomed or supported or loved."

The look Josh gave Hope was unmissable. A light elbow in Nick's side confirmed that Dylan saw it too. A swell of happiness for his friends filled Nick's spirit, and he drew a long breath as he watched Pastor Walker lead Josh through the baptismal vows and then into the waters of the font.

From the water, Josh motioned for Hope to join him. With a smile, Nick stood with the rest of the church body as Josh was lowered into the water and drawn back up. Peace radiated from the man's face as he threw his arms around Pastor Walker and then shared a lingering embrace with Hope.

Just then four ladies began singing 'The Cleansing Wave' in a gentle acapella, while Pastor Walker motioned for Josh and Hope to step out of the font and into the deacons' room off to the right of the stage. Nick retook his seat with the church body and clasped his hands over his thighs while he listened to the closing hymn. He could hear the soft blowing of noses and chuckles as collective emotions needed to be released. Baptismal services were special, but there was an extra significance to this one.

Great changes were coming – he felt a stirring within him, unsettling and exciting. But was it for him, or for someone else?

CHAPTER TWENTY-ONE

The loud clang of weights falling back into place reverberated across the room at The Valley Gymnasium. Nick didn't often work the weights bench, preferring the bike or treadmill, but tonight he felt that he needed more than his usual routine.

Thoughts about Alice not being right for him had settled in his head since the baptism yesterday. Until then, he'd held out hope that she'd come around – like Josh did. But yesterday that hope had slipped away. Troubled, he worked the pec deck in roughly, his focus glued to a grimy spot on the carpet before him.

A towel slap to his chest broke his concentration and Nick let the weights clang back into place, turning a fiery glare to Dylan who stood next to him. While he knew the gesture was good-natured, and he'd normally play back, tonight he just couldn't. He unhooked his arms from the pads and rose from the seat. "It's all yours, big fella."

"What's eating you tonight, man?"

Nick sat at the lateral raise and hung his arms off the bar. He knew a hard workout wouldn't move the funk he was in. Only prayer would do that. Although he already felt the heavy answer to his question, it conflicted with what he wanted. Sighing a heavy sigh, he looked square at Dylan. "I am going to break up with Alice."

Dylan wrapped his towel around the back of his neck and grimaced. Nick read his look. It wasn't one of pretend sympathies – Dylan was feeling the heaviness he was. Nick rose and moved with Dylan back to continue the conversation near where Trent was on the treadmill. Trent slowed his run to a brisk walk, and his expression was one of curiosity. "What's this about Alice?"

Nick explained, "her family will be moving in a few weeks. She's staying here for me, to give us a go. I can't ask her to stay if I'm starting to feel that we're not right for each other."

"What's brought this on?" Dylan stepped closer; his voice hushed against the din of the gym. "I had you two picked for an engagement any day."

Nick gave a derisive snort. Then, leaning against the power tower, he nodded slowly. "I have come close to asking her, but something seems to stop me. I know we're not on the same page when it comes to matters of God, but then I took Josh as encouragement that one day she'd come around like he did. Then yesterday at the baptism, listening to Josh's testimony, an impression came to mind that Alice isn't ready yet. I one hundred percent feel it was God speaking to me to let her go with her family."

"Does it have to be a breakup? Dylan offered. "What about long-distance?"

"Across two states?" Nick shook his head. "Maybe if we both had nine to five, Monday to Friday jobs. But with our timetables, it would be quite a juggling act just to keep in touch."

Trent had slowed his workout further to a leisurely stroll. "As hard as it would be, being apart could be exactly what Alice needs for the seeds you've planted to grow. God is a God of relationships, remember that, and maybe some space would give her time to seek Him."

"Five bucks says she doesn't see it that way." Nick shot Trent a humorless grin before turning his gaze to adjust his wristwatch. "More likely she'll blame God."

The treadmill stopped and Nick looked up to see Trent step down from the mat and approach him. A big brother like expression lit the man's features as he rested a hand upon Nick's shoulders. "That may be, but it's God's time to be with her – and, with you."

* * * *

The front door buzzer sounded, and Nick looked up from his desk to see who had entered the station. A young mum stood at the counter jigging a baby on her hip while appearing to scold a toddler at her feet. Nick looked over the mounting paperwork on his desk then pushed himself up from his seat, making his way towards the reception area.

Fifteen minutes later Nick watched the young woman leave, ushering the toddler through the door before her while the baby on her hip had her eyes locked on him. He waved. Then caught himself and turned his attention back to the daybook before him, recording the woman's lost phone details.

Did he just wave at a baby?

Nick chuckled to himself as he shut the book, then left the reception area and went back to his desk. The kid was cute. Full of innocence. It was refreshing.

"Marshall." Greg called out, as Nick passed his desk. "You got that paperwork done yet?"

"Not yet, sir." Nick retook the seat at his desk and suppressed a yawn. "Without interruptions, I should have it done before home time."

Ignoring his empty coffee cup, Nick pulled out the paper he was working on and focused his mind back on the job. The Academy had warned them of the amount of paperwork that was involved in this line of work, and that time management was a huge discipline. While he was good at time management, he couldn't deny he was starting to feel the strain – even with these rostered correspondence shifts dedicated to getting paperwork done, interruptions still meant the deskwork was never finished. Commitments at church were pulling at him, but he didn't want to let that go to compensate for the workload. He would just have to dig deep and draw more out of himself. He yawned again, blinked and focused in on the database in front of him. It would all be Ok. If he could hold out another two years, then he could put in for a transfer to The Valley and cut out his travel time.

The rattle of chair wheels broke his concentration, and Nick looked up to see Geoff had pulled a chair to join him at his desk. Nick put his pen down and faced his superior. "What can I do for you, sir?"

"You look wrung out, Officer Marshall."

Surprised by the blunt delivery, Nick coughed into his fist. Despite the hard look in Geoff's eyes, the man appeared to be genuinely interested; he'd brought the chair over to Nick's desk after all. He was up for a chat. "I'm doing ok."

"Is there a particular case playing on your mind? Do you need another meeting with your peer support officer?"

"No, I am coping well enough thanks Geoff. It's just the traveling and external commitments that are starting to tire me out." Nick tried to sound upbeat.

Geoff laid an elbow on the corner of Nick's desk and rested his chin in between his thumb and pointer finger. "The first few years of an officer's training are critical, and the ongoing nature of the job requires an officer to be functioning at a hundred percent. Can you postpone some of these external commitments or pass the baton, so-to-speak?"

A warning flashed in Nick's mind. He'd seen his friends face similar circumstances and he had promised himself God would come first. He would honor his commitment to the church and youth group, and trust God to take care of the rest. He shook his head. "Not really, Sir. The only way I see time freeing up for me is eventually transferring to a station closer to home."

Geoff sat forward and gave Nick a slap on the shoulder. "Well, if everything is ok, I'd better let you get back to it. Don't forget to de-kit before you head off."

Nick chuckled at the reference to Eddie once leaving work with his kit still on. He'd driven ten minutes down the road before realizing, then had to turn back to the station. With a shake of his head, Nick went back to the paperwork before him.

They were right at the Academy; the paperwork really did never end.

CHAPTER TWENTY-TWO

"How's your day been, beautiful?"

Nick rested his forearms along the railing of the outdoor entertaining area that overlooked the back lawn, listening to the soothing richness in Alice's voice come down the phone as she recounted her day. While she talked, a sadness began to weave its way into his mind and erased the smile on his face.

He didn't want to end their relationship – and she had no idea it was coming.

The evening was balmy, with a light breeze that ruffled the tree canopies, and causing the citronella lanterns hanging from the rafters around him to flicker. The air felt charged. It was the kind of night he'd love to go for a walk along the beach with Alice or hang out together at her family home. Or even invite her over for a quiet dinner under the stars.

Lost in fantasy of how a dinner for two might end, Nick realized he'd tuned out. He snapped back to attention, but she'd busted him.

"You're not listening, are you?"

Nick chuckled. "I'm sorry. It's your voice. It draws me into some sort of lull."

"Oh really?"

Nick grinned as he straightened and moved around the deck, hearing the purr within her dulcet voice. "Yes, really."

"Tell me about your day then, handsome."

"It was very long and tiring. And not that interesting. I'd rather listen to you than my own voice."

"Well, you can be a bit monotone."

"That's just my policeman voice, I'll have you know, Miss."

Alice laughed, drawing a chuckle from him also. Oh, he didn't want to end their relationship, but what Trent had said was playing over in his mind…

'It's God's time to be with her – and, with you.'

The timber railing was rough under his touch as Nick ran a hand along its length, thinking. He cleared his throat. "Are you busy tonight?"

"Not really. I was going to turn in shortly. I'm on earlies this week. You? Are you and Eddie going to stay up watching shoot-em-ups, snuggled on the couch?"

The giggle that followed Alice's intentionally razzing comment caused Nick to lose his train of thought. "Ah. No, we prefer more the science fiction type, you know, like romantic comedies."

"Hey!"

"Kidding." Nick chuckled. Envisaging her playful punch if he'd said that to her face, he pulled the conversation back on track. "But hey, I would like to talk to you about something, and I'd rather do it in person."

"And you want to talk tonight? Ok. You'd better come over with chocolate or something then."

A sorrowful grin lifted the edge of Nick's mouth.

Or something.

He sniffed. "I'll be there in twenty minutes."

* * * *

The evening air streaming through the air vents in Nick's car began to smell like eucalyptus as he drew closer to the hills of Briardale.

The biggest chocolate bar from the local supermarket sat on the seat next to him, while the words he wanted to say tumbled around heavily within his mind. "God, help me. Am I doing the right thing?" Nick murmured as he pulled into Alice's family home. The For-Sale sign had a SOLD sticker across the middle, driving home the finality of the family's move.

Hesitancy nipped at his conscience as he looked at the front entrance, illuminated by the porch light Alice had left on for him.

Maybe they could try the long-distance thing? At least with long-distance they would have their time apart – God could have His time with her, as Trent put it – and they could also spend time together when their schedules aligned. It could work.

It could.

Just then, the door opened, and Alice's silhouette appeared in the doorway. *Here we go.* Nick coached himself before stepping out of his car.

"Shall we go inside for this important visit, or…?" Alice left the sentence hang as she strolled down the driveway towards him. Nick rested against the bonnet of his car and held a hand towards her.

Alice's hand slipped into his and she tucked herself next to him against his car. "What's on your mind, Nick?"

Her hand was full of strength and warmth. Surely they just fit together? "Us. We should have a talk."

Uncertainty flashed through her eyes; her voice became hushed. "Ok. What is it?"

"I think you should go with your folks. When they move, you should go."

A breeze swept up the drive and lifted the edges of her hair – the only part of her that moved while her unblinking gaze began to harden. "You know my family is leaving in less than two weeks?"

"Yeah."

"And you drop this on me now."

Nick gave her hand a light squeeze. "It's not ideal timing. I know."

Alice let out a curt laugh and looked away. "No. It's not." She withdrew her hand, and Nick grimaced as he watched her stare back at the family home.

"I needed to talk to you about this. It's been on my mind." Nick pushed himself off his car and stood to face her. In the amber light coming from the porch, he'd never seen her appear so vulnerable. "I'm concerned that you're staying for us, but I'm not sure where we are going at this point in time. We have strong differing opinions on some major issues."

Alice shot him a bored look. "Well, you still need some work."

Nick breathed a chuckle at Alice's attempted humor and gave a nod of his head. "I'll take that."

Alice pushed off the bonnet of the car and stepped into him. Taking his hands, she gave them a light shake. "Yes, we disagree, but it's nothing so big that I didn't think we couldn't work through…"

Nick interrupted, "and I would love to keep working on these things, don't get me wrong. But I'm trying to anticipate what will be the best thing for us. What if you stay, and we can't work things out?"

"What if I stay and we *do* work things out?"

The grin on Alice's face and teasing tone in her voice derailed Nick's train of thought. "I'm trying to be serious here."

Alice tilted her head as she gazed back at him, her eyes like large pools of molten gold reflecting the soft porch light. "Did you think you'd just rock up here, and I'd agree to this?" The combination of plea and hope shining back at him was an alluring and tempting combination and he found himself faltering. He took a small step back, though kept a hold of her hands. "No. But I need you to consider it. I know you're due to move in with your friends in two weeks also, so this gives time for them to find someone else. You have time to really think about what our future looks like if you stay. I'm not going to change, Alice. I still want you, but I want God and His plans for me above that. And as much as I want you to be beside me at church, I cannot force you and I don't want to."

The front door opened and Nick glanced over his shoulder as Mr. Knight appeared on the porch. "You kids coming in?"

"Nah." Alice called back. Her voice was chipper, but Nick heard the strain behind her words. "Nick's about to head off."

"Didn't you just arrive, son?"

The look of curiosity that crossed Mr. Knights features wasn't missed. Nick nodded as he turned to face Alice's dad. "Yes sir, it was just a quick visit."

There was a pause before Mr. Knight turned back to the house. There was clearly more that he wanted to say, but Nick was glad he had withheld his thoughts and left them to it. He looked back at Alice. "I'm about to head off, am I?"

The coolness in Alice's eyes when she looked at him, felt like the metal of his Smith & Wesson against his skin. She had her no-nonsense glare on as if she had just pulled him over for speeding. "Well, aren't you?"

Surprised by the change in her demeanor, he straightened. "Not until we agree on where we're headed. I don't want to leave here with things the way they are."

Alice drew in a long breath and lifted a shoulder. "Seems to me Nick, that you'd come here to deliver the mail, not discuss it. What do you want me to say?"

"When we spoke on the beach, you suggested trying long-distance. I'm not suggesting a breakup, I'm saying let's try long-distance." Alice turned away with a sniff. Nick grasped her shoulders and turned her back to him. The defiant lock of her jaw began to soften as her eyes searched his. Nick nodded, hoping to encourage the hopeful look he saw in her eyes. A slow smile began to creep along her mouth.

"Yeah?"

"Yeah." Leaning towards her, Nick kissed the tip of her nose. Her breath puffed out on a laugh, and she tossed her hair as she threw her head back. "Oh, I thought you were breaking up with me."

A lightness filled Nick's heart, and he beamed back at Alice when she looked at him, linking her arms around the back of his neck. "I was struggling with the idea of my family moving two states away and you've just taken a massive burden off my mind."

Wrapping his arms around her waist, Nick ran a hand over her back. The silky-smooth cotton of the light T-shirt she wore teased his sense of touch. "I thought you were happy with wanting to stay?"

"I was. But you were right, I was only staying for you. I was starting to worry, though, that the pull of wanting to be with my family would cause resentment towards you." With surprising strength Alice pulled his head down and whispered against his mouth. "And I didn't want that."

The back of her T-shirt balled in Nick's hands as he held her against him. Her fingertips light against the back of his neck, the taste of her lips, and the subtle sweetness of her perfume drew him deeper until he forgot his surroundings.

A flashing light broke into Nick's subconscious disturbing his utopia and awareness broke like the dawn – they were in the driveway of Alice's family home. He pulled back and turned towards the intrusive beam to see a silhouette standing in the doorway. Alice's mum was flicking the porch light on and off! Alice's hands slipped from around his neck and trailed down his chest; he looked back at her.

"Alright you two." Mrs. Knight's no-nonsense voice barked at them. "Miss, you have an early start tomorrow. I suggest you get to bed."

Alice sighed, looking past Nick to where her mum stood. "Ok Mum. I'll be there in just a minute." When she looked back at him, Nick swallowed. Suddenly he didn't want her to go with her parents. He'd back-pedaled on the breakup he had come to do, and now he felt he was about to do the same with agreeing to be long-distance. He needed her here.

"Thank you," Alice said, her voice a husky whisper. Then, with a lithe sidestep, she moved out from between him and his car and began to head back towards the house. Nick turned to watch her and she turned back to him to wave. "See you tomorrow? I'm leaving in two weeks, remember?"

Nick gave a slow nod. "See you tomorrow, beautiful. Sweet dreams."

CHAPTER
TWENTY-THREE

"Marshall. Look sharp, kid."

Nick looked up from the sentencing paperwork he was working on for tomorrow's hearing, to see Geoff lean against his cubical wall and take a sip from the mug in his hand. "For what, sir?"

"Vera Waltham is visiting our station today. She's the bigwig down at The Valley Headquarters and first impressions are vital – don't let her see you tired and not 100% focused on the job, ok?"

The office room chatter and ringing phones faded to the background as Nick concentrated on what Geoff wasn't saying. If he hoped to transfer to The Valley one day, he needed to leave a good impression today. Nick clicked his pen a few times then leaned towards Geoff, keeping his voice low. "Yes, Sir. Best behavior."

"Geoff, have you got a moment?"

Before Nick could put words to his racing thoughts, one of the senior officers from the station pulled Geoff aside for a hushed conversation. With feigned focus, Nick turned his attention back to the paperwork he was working on. His peripheral picked up the two men moving towards the meeting cubicles at the back of the room.

Unable to keep his thoughts on the job, Nick flicked his pen onto his desk and sat back in his chair. The look on the two officers' faces were serious. They glanced in his direction. Did they have new information about Jack's case? Remembering Geoff's earlier words of advice, Nick turned back to his work. He had to stay focused.

* * * *

"Saw you and the big boss lady having a good chin wag." Eddie said, glancing at Nick from where he knelt before the BBQ gas bottle. "What was that about?"

Nick ripped open the bag of meat Eddie had bought from the butcher, pulled out the lamb chops and chicken kebabs, then laid them on the tray beside the BBQ. The evening was balmy, and cicadas were filling the night air with their almost deafening chirps. He glanced at Eddie. "Yeah. You know those times when something is happening and you don't really believe that it is?"

"Just about every day." Eddie stood and clicked the fire lighter a couple of times before a whoomph announced the BBQ had started. In moments, the air was filled with the scent of burning charcoal and fat left over from last time they'd cooked.

Nick opened one of the bottles of sparkling grape juice that Dave had given him at the last leadership team meeting, and he poured himself a glass. He heard Eddie snort just as a hiss from an opening beer can sounded. "Can't believe you drink that. Why don't you have a real drink?"

"You don't want to lock horns with me over what alcohol does to your body, mate."

"Can't be worse than that carbonated sugary drink, could it?"

Nick felt the corner of his mouth hitch. Without a word, he grasped the neck of the bottle and held it to his housemate. Eddie raised an eyebrow, took the bottle off him and read the label. A moment later, Eddie replaced the bottle on the outdoor table behind them, turned back to the BBQ and cleared his throat. "Anyway, you were about to tell me what happened today."

"I was in the kitchen making a coffee when Waltham comes in with Geoff. He introduces me, we speak briefly about how I went at the Academy and how I'm settling in at Richmond station." Nick took a sip of his drink then swirled the deep purple liquid around his glass. "Then, she asked me some questions about my relationship with Jack. Something about it felt odd, but I went with the flow. Then she wrapped up the conversation with some other inane questions, shook my hand and left."

The BBQ hissed and spat as Eddie flopped the lamb chops onto the grill.

"I just feel something is at play that I don't know about." Nick ripped open a bag of chips, sat at the outdoor table and stretched his legs out. "I watched her walk away with Geoff feeling like I was in trouble or something."

A hinge screeched inside the house, catching Nick's attention and he looked over his shoulder to see Alice step out to the outdoor area. He rose from his seat, holding an arm out to her, and she slipped into his side. Eddie had a pensive look on his face as he clicked the tongs in a distracted manner.

"What are you thinking Ed?" Nick ventured, curiosity winning over.

Eddie gave a shake of his head and turned to look back at him. "I don't know. But I'm as interested in what's cookin' as you are."

CHAPTER TWENTY-FOUR

"Heads up!"

Nick halted just inside the door of Dave's library at the warning. Just then, one of the many pillows from the pew under the window cuffed him across the head as it flew past. With a casual glance, he looked to where the Christmas-themed pillow now lay on the floor beside him.

"Oh, sorry Nick, I thought it was Trent." Lexi grinned from behind her hand. Beside her Hope coughed a laugh. "Hun, he'd have known it was coming and ducked."

Nick felt his eyes narrow on Hope as she rummaged through her bag. "Testing him, are we?"

Hope glanced up and winked at him. Nick held her gaze as he bent to retrieve the pillow and tossed it over to Dylan. While

Dylan and Lexi didn't say anything, he didn't miss the question that flashed across Lexi's face. Had Hope said something to Lexi?

"Good to see you man," Dylan said, breaking his line of thought. "How'd you go with Alice the other night?"

A grin curled on Nick's face as he crossed his arms and settled into the pew seat beside Dylan. He was still feeling good about the decision he'd made. Something within him knew that God was going to do something amazing in their time apart. "Yeah… she's going to go with her folks and we're going to try the long-distance thing."

Just then Dave and Trent entered the room. Nick lifted his chin in greeting to them just as he felt Dylan rap his thigh. "That is great news. I thought a breakup was a bit extreme. Distance will give you both room to work out if your differences can be overcome."

"I like Alice," Hope added, "I'll be praying that the long-distance thing will work out for both of you."

"When we feel impressed by the Lord about something, we need to carry it out to the letter."

Nick's grin froze as he turned to Trent. What he'd said had caught the room's attention – conversations ceased and he felt all eyes on Trent now settled in his usual seat at the back of the room.

"What aren't you saying there, mate?" asked Nick.

"Deviation from what the Lord asks only ends in hurt and disappointment – for us."

The warning behind what Trent said sent a sprinkle of goosebumps up Nick's arms. If Trent wasn't who he was starting to think he was, he'd have argued back. But, as he held Trent's gaze, he sensed a dark cloud gathering over his relationship with Alice. But why? What? Had he made the wrong decision? He gave a cool shrug as he uncrossed his arms and sat forward. "Noted." Then, turning to Dave, he changed the topic. "Dave, what's the plan for this week?"

"Oh, hey guys," Hope sat forward on her seat, her arm up like she was asking for permission to speak in class. "Before we jump into this week's agenda, I need to let you know that I won't be around. I received a call on my way in about assisting a dental crew headed to Vanuatu on Wednesday. I'm so excited, but nervous at the same time. Can you all pray for me, please?"

Dave looked to be making a note. "Not a problem Hope, will do. Any other prayer requests before we start?"

Dylan cleared his throat and asked for prayer over a project his footy club had started with a troubled public school, then Lexi requested prayers over her end-of-year exams.

Nick ran a hand over his hair, as his concerns over something brewing at work came back to mind, then he rested his elbow on the back of the pew. "Yeah, I have something I'd like prayers over too. I had a meeting today about how I'm settling in, and I feel in my gut something is wrong – even though the meeting was easy and amicable, I feel something is up."

Nick looked around the room at his friends' focused expressions all trained on him. Dave wrote something else down before he looked back at him. "Nick, the Holy Spirit speaks into our subconscious. If you're feeling something isn't right, there is a high chance something isn't. As long as I've known you, you've had a great way of reading situations and people, so don't stop listening to it now. Ok?"

Dave rubbed a hand over his mouth and looked to be deep in thought. Nick felt his eyes narrow as he watched the body language of his youth minister. With a sharp inhale, Dave straightened in his seat; his palms flat on his desk before him. "Before we get down to business, I have some news to share. I'm going to be heading back to America…"

The atmosphere withdrew like the outgoing of the tide. Hearing Dave speak about the phone call he had received and the decision he and Linda had made to return to his hometown, made the team feel like their foundation was about to be knocked out from under them. Nick made a study of his hands as Dave continued. The man was like a second dad to him and had been for many years. He'd counseled him, coached him, shepherded him, and now he was leaving. Nick gave a shake of his head and looked up. Dave was looking back at him and Nick held his gaze.

He wasn't ready for this to end; he wasn't ready for his mentor to leave.

What would happen to the leadership team?

* * * *

"I cannot believe he's leaving." Lexi's voice was soft as she toyed with the Christmas-themed napkin on the table at The Mariners Inn.

The mood had fallen flat at Dave's after his announcement, and the night had wound up fast. Dave had the end-of-year windup all sorted out and handed the details to them on slips of paper. It was like he knew that after he dropped the bomb on them there would be no energy to discuss the upcoming evening, so he had it all planned and ready to go.

The balcony table they liked to occupy was vacant and, without a word, they'd sunk into their seats. Silence settled over them like a wet blanket. A stark contrast to the merry jingling of Christmas carols playing in the background.

Nick watched Dylan put an arm around Lexi, tuck her into his side and press a kiss to her temple. Lowering his gaze to his untouched drink, Nick toyed with his glass of ice water and watched the smearing water marks it left behind on the table. He felt like his world was shifting rapidly.

A tinkle of ice cubes drew his attention to Hope beside him, as she took a sip from her water. She put the glass down and sighed. It wasn't often he saw her without her perpetual high-on-life attitude, but she looked as somber as the rest of them.

"This isn't the end." Trent's voice felt like a warm embrace and Nick looked over at him. "God moves His people around all the time, like in a game of chess. Dave moving on does not signal the end of anything, but the next chapter in an incredible masterpiece God is weaving."

"What will happen to the leadership team though, Trent?" Hope asked. There was a note of vulnerability in her voice that, combined with the plea behind her eyes as she looked across the table at Trent, caused a momentary clash of instincts. Normally Nick would give her a jab on the arm and quip something along the lines of toughening up, so, the desire to comfort her instead unnerved him. He cleared his throat as he drew his drink to his mouth. "We'll be fine, Meyer."

"God will provide a leader."

Nick exchanged a look with Trent over the rim of his glass. He heard Dylan and Lexi reassuring Hope, but there was something behind Trent's eyes that held Nick's gaze. An assurance that God would provide a leader and that everything would be ok reverberated within his mind. Did Trent *say* that... to him?

A message tone came from his back pocket and, tearing his eyes away from Trent, Nick pulled his phone out to check who'd messaged. A frown crinkled his forehead seeing a message from Dave.

'Nick. There's something I'd like to discuss with you. Free tomorrow?'

CHAPTER
TWENTY - FIVE

The morning was bright and fresh after a light rain had crossed The Valley during the night. Nick breathed deep of the salty sea breeze that mingled with the sweet eucalyptus coming from the bush nearby.

It was odd for Dave to request Nick to have a meeting with him during the week – usually they'd meet after leadership meeting or youth night, so already he was detecting something suspicious.

The door was open when Nick stepped up to the porch and he peered through the fly screen.

"G'day Dave." Nick rapped a couple times on the doorframe then waited to see if Dave answered. When no one appeared, Nick stepped down from the porch and made his way around the back. Perhaps the man was weeding his veggie patch or picking peaches from his orchard.

The latch lifted easily under a finger and Nick let himself in to the backyard. He could see Dave's legs peeking out from under one of his peach trees. Nick sidled up to the tree, admiring the ruby red blush over the fruit. "G'day Dave. Great looking harvest you got going here."

"Help yourself." Dave's voice came from within the fruit-laden branches. "There's plenty to go around."

"I'll do you one better," Nick grabbed a nearby basket, "I'll help you pick." Moving to the next tree, Nick lifted the mesh for keeping the birds off and started lightly twisting the delicate fruit off the branches. "So, Dave, what did you want to discuss with me? Or was this a ploy to get some help picking fruit?"

A grin spread upon Nick's face hearing the chuckle come from under the tree Dave was working at. "No, son. I want to put something to you."

There was a different rustling sound coming from Dave's direction and Nick looked over his shoulder to see Dave appearing from under the tree and working his way out of the netting that covered it. He put down the basket he was holding and looked at Nick. Nick held his gaze for a moment, his hand still working off ripe peaches from the branch. Then, reading what was unsaid, Nick put down his own basket and joined his youth minister in the morning sunshine. This looked as though it was going to be a serious conversation, and an odd feeling of unease came over him as he waited for Dave to start talking.

"I'm not going to beat around the bush here. When I head off, I'd like you to step up and continue the leadership team."

Nick held Dave's unwavering stare. A myriad of thoughts and questions flashed through his mind, none of which he could grasp. He let out his breath, chuckled, and rubbed the back of his neck. Dave took a step towards him and placed a hand on his shoulder. "I know what this is asking of you – you're almost a year into a long-desired career and you've settled into the routine and discipline that it requires. To accept would mean leaving that behind and letting God plot you a whole new course – the question is, would you be willing to let Him do that?"

A gentle breeze ruffled the leaves of the trees around him as Nick continued to hold Dave's eyes and a weight began to form upon his shoulders. When Dave removed his hand, the weight remained – it was not a physical weight.

It was a weight of expectation.

Duty.

A calling.

Nick dropped his head and turned away. Thoughts, too many to count, flashed through his mind and he had no idea how to answer the unspoken question. He turned. "You're leaving before Easter, aren't you?"

At the slow dip of Dave's head, Nick looked away again. "And you, or God I should say, is asking – no wait that's not right, is expecting, me to step in?" Nick turned back to Dave. "I'm a police officer, albeit a junior one. I'm not a youth minister."

"The Bible is full of stories about those who thought they were ill-equipped for the job God called them to." Dave stepped towards him. "Moses, Gideon, Esther... the Disciples."

Dave's gazed locked on and Nick felt the intensity of his words. His chest began to tighten. Peaches forgotten; Nick shook his head. "Dave, look. I ah. I'll need time to think about this and, of course, pray about it. I mean, like you said, I've just started a career..."

"Are you sure that this career is what God has prepared you for?"

Nick straightened. He'd never been so sure of something in his life. "Of course. I've always known I wanted to be a police officer. I'd have enrolled into the Academy straight out of high school if Dad didn't insist I get some life experience behind me first. I know I have a gift of service, never a shred of doubt... 'though, some doubt is making itself known now." Nick felt a deep frown sink into his forehead as he looked down at the lush lawn at his feet. Yes, his gift was service...

"Nick."

Nick looked back at his youth minister. There was a gentleness behind his shrewd eyes that reminded him of his dad when he was about to teach him a life lesson. Aware of his increasing heart rate, Nick pocketed his hands and tried to focus his mind on absorbing what Dave was going to say.

"Service is a broad stroke of the brush – how do you know it specifically means as a police officer? From where I'm standing, I would question it for reasons being: your placement is in a station you didn't want, the awkward working hours mean you're tired all the time but your character still demands you must continue commitments acquired before-hand... the first first-responder incident you attended has been, and I believe still is, proving hard for your mind to process... shall I continue?"

"Touché." Nick acknowledged the points his youth minister had made, then looked back over to the tree next to him. He reached up and twisted a peach off, weighing it in his hands as he glanced at Dave. "Nah, you don't need to continue." He bit into the peach and savored the juicy sweetness of the summertime fruit in the warmth of the sun. Peace flashed through his mind and for a blissful moment not a worry existed.

He caught sight of Dave in his peripheral and a stiffness once again took hold of his muscles. He turned.

"It's possible that God is preparing you for something greater, Nick. Over the years I've watched you grow, and you've always known yourself. The stability and consistency you bring to the team overflows and the youth see it. You're a terrific role model and man of God. Take some time to pray about it and let me know. The Conference can help you out with education and allowances." Dave paused then clasped his hands in a prayer gesture. "Many of us don't continue in the career we started out in. It's not a sign of failure, just stepping stones on the journey."

CHAPTER TWENTY - SIX

The buttery scent of popcorn enticed Nick as he stepped into the bustling vestibule of the city's Laser Zone center. He headed towards his group, weaving around the throngs of people underneath the red and green tinsel, nutcracker statues and a giant Santa sleigh that hung from the roof.

Dave was handing out tickets when Nick arrived. The youths were separated into three teams, with two leaders per team and Nick was meant to be paired up with Josh, since Hope was away on a mission trip.

Nearby, double doors banged open and a room full of laser tag players spilled out into the foyer. The obvious laughter and conversations the players were sharing was lost in the din of the contemporary Christmas carols playing over the sound system. Nick shared a look with Dylan and Lexi – It was not their choice of Christmas music.

"Hey guys!" Josh appeared beside Nick. "Sorry about taking things down to the wire, but I had to finish a phone call in the car. My sister wants to do Bible studies!"

Nick chuckled as he shook Josh's hand. "That is great news!"

"She looked moved by your baptism." Dylan added, shaking the man's hand in greeting.

Another door opened and more youths spilled out like a wave crashing upon the beach. As soon as the crowd had cleared, Dylan and Lexi began shepherding their group in. An attendant closed the doors behind them.

"Hey Nick," a young man named Michael sidled up to him. "Can we buddy up with you tonight?" Nick grinned at Michael and the two other boys with him. They weren't more than fifteen. "What's your plan, Mike?" Nick pocketed his hands.

"To win!" Craig said, stepping closer to speak over the music. "Tony and his friends say they're going to target us first to get us out."

"Ah. And you boys think that what happens in there is like what I do out in the real world?" Nick tipped his head towards the exit and smirked at the young boys before him. "This is laser tag, boys. It's like dodgeball but instead of a ball, we have a laser. Not quite like what I do for a living."

The game attendant began to give their group the run-down of the rules: twenty minutes of play, the first team to the marker wins. Next thing Nick knew was another game attendant was moving around them handing out laser tag blasters. Nick weighed the blaster in his hands and smirked at Josh. "You ready?"

Josh mimed clicking his gun and dipped his head. "Let's show these kids how it's done."

Suddenly, the starting buzzer rang and the youths thundered past them like a herd of brumbies. They disappeared amongst the strobing, multi-colored laser lights into the warehouse-styled play area. Nick paused at the doorway, assessed the room, then crouch ran towards a pile of florescence paint-splatted tires. So much for Mike's plea to stick together, he thought with a sardonic grin as he peered around his cover. He couldn't even see Josh's giant form in the disco-like room any more. Music blared, lights flickered, laughter and squeals ran out all around him... but there was a mission to complete: get to the marker.

Staying crouched, Nick moved along the wall – keeping his blaster up and eye on the scope, taking out a few targets as he went.

Once he had found the L-shaped obstacle he'd spied from the tires, Nick changed his angle. Some of the youths had noticed him and had shot at him but there was no way these kids were going to take him out. A quick glance over his shoulder revealed an aqua-illuminated corner-looking room. It would be risky revealing himself by ducking in there, but to win the game all areas must be checked out. Blaster at the ready, Nick moved quickly towards the corner room.

Clear.

He crept around the corner and out the other side. To his left, a darkened ramp with orange, fluorescent trims lead to the second floor. Before him, room dividers flashed with edges of green, yellow and blue. To his right paint-splattered barrels were stacked two high. Choosing the ramp, Nick surveyed his run to make sure it was clear, then with quick feet started to move. Hearing his name shouted and a quick succession of lasers hitting the ramp walls just behind him, he just reached the top in time. He dive-rolled in behind another room divider and regained his bearings – and breath.

"Ten minutes left on the clock."

Nick turned sharply to his side to see Josh crouched and peering through his scope around the other side of the divider. "Located the marker yet?"

"Negative."

Nick turned back to look out his side of the divider, lined up some targets and took them out. "Any sign of Mike and his guys?"

"Taken out, early in the game."

"They should have waited for our cover." Disappointed to think the boys were out of the game, Nick continued to search from his position for the marker. He could see half a dozen youths in a standoff nearby, any minute they'd drop like flies. He glanced at Josh. "Any idea how many are left in the game?"

"Nope. Hard to see anything in these flickering lights."

Nick glanced around their position. The players were thinning out fast – or more were learning tactile play and not to run around like headless chickens. He looked at his watch. Five minutes to go. The coast was clear to make a dash to the nearest pile of paint-splattered tires.

Suddenly, movement to Nick's right snapped his attention around. A youth he couldn't identify because of the strobe light above, held a blaster pointed at them. Instinct kicked in and Nick was on his feet, in front of Josh, blaster trained back at the youth.

His vest illuminated and the youth ran off.

He was out of the game.

CHAPTER
TWENTY - SEVEN

The clink of glasses tinkled and muffled cheers and cat calls of encouragement rang out as Nick and his friends settled at a table in the Laser Zone's café. Laughter mingled with upbeat Christmas carols and the buzzing, zinging, bleeping that came from the arcade area.

"And that's another year done, guys!" Lexi sang moments before she took a sip of her tall iced tea.

"Can you believe we've done two years already?" Dylan placed his glass of water on the table and sat back in his seat. "What a way to finish the year, though."

Trent chuckled. "I think they all thought we'd go easy on them."

Still feeling sore over being bested by one of the youths, Nick took a sip of his espresso and nodded as they exchanged stories of how their games played out. So far, no youths had come by to brag, so he was still none-the-wiser as to who took him out of the game.

A rap on his back drew his mind off his musing and to Trent who sat beside him, a tickled expression on his face. "Nick, stop trying to figure out who beat you in the game, and join us in the present."

Before Nick could respond, laughter broke out between Josh and Dylan, and he looked across the table at them. Dylan was rapping Josh's back. "Who'd have thought you'd end up on this path, brother?"

Josh raised his eyebrows. "Never in a hundred years. I've got a Zoom Bible study with some fellas from the Tigers club tomorrow!"

Nick watched the conversation playing out with interest. "Well, we know that God knows us better than we know ourselves. He knows where we will find most joy and satisfaction in life."

Even as he said the words to encourage Josh, he felt they could apply to him. Was God calling him into ministry?

He shook his head. He could minister to people as a police officer, couldn't he?

"So, who's up for Christmas Carols on the foreshore next week?" Dylan voice broke into the troubling thoughts racing through Nick's mind. Nick replaced his glass on the table. "I'm on lates all next week, so I'm out."

"I'm in." Lexi raised a hand as she took a sip from her drink.

"I'll be there." Josh added.

"What time does your shift start on the Saturday night?" Trent said and Nick turned to him. "I start at 7p.m."

Trent gave a dip of his head as he reached for his glass of water.

"It'll be the first time I've missed the lighting of the Christmas Tree." Nick downed his drink. The reality of what he'd said sank in. There were so many sacrifices being a police offi-cer, but the pros still outweighed the cons. He loved serving. He loved helping. He loved the protection he could offer and the constant learning.

"But maybe I could get Geoff to swing by during our evening patrol."

* * * *

"So, I just realized you're on nights and I'm on days this week?"

Nick rubbed his forehead as he frowned into the phone. He knew what Alice was saying. "Yeah. Not the way I was expecting to spend your last week here."

Alice's disappointment was palpable. Nick imagined she was pacing her bedroom, the house empty except for the necessary furniture and plane tickets pinned on the family corkboard ready for this coming Thursday night.

"Well, I guess we spend our last week together texting or talking on the phone. How romantic."

A rare moment of silence fell over the conversation and Nick stretched out on his bed. "Let's call it a preview for how things will be for us going forward, only, it starts a week earlier than expected."

A humorless chuckle came down the line. "Trust you to find the silver lining in anything." Alice's voice was flat, and Nick was about to offer some encouragement when she cleared her throat.

"You know though, Nick, last night was our last night when our ships weren't passing in the dark and you chose to spend it with your church youth group. Where does that leave me?"

Nick tucked an arm behind his head and searched his ceiling as he considered how to answer. He hadn't even questioned what to do, he just intrinsically knew what came first – service to God.

That would not go over well.

"Nick?"

"Yeah, I'm here." Nick answered Alice's inquiring voice. Somewhere in the back of his mind he felt, no matter how he worded it, it was not going to land well in Alice's mind. "Last night wasn't free for me. I had a commitment to honor."

"An end of year youth break-up?" Alice's voice was low and held a note of contempt. "You weren't even required to be there, as I understand."

"Technically, we're not required to be there each week either. It's a volunteer role, which you know I take seriously."

A long sigh answered his comment, and he felt a heavy weight begin to swirl in his gut. "Having said that, I take us seriously too…"

Soft laughter interrupted him and Nick paused, leaving the sentence hanging. She was disappointed and made sure he knew it. He cleared his throat. "I do, Alice. I also understand why you feel the way you do. Sometime this week, I know there will be some time we can see each other before you leave."

"Does it involve, someone chucking a sickie?"

"Not on my end." Happy to hear the levity creep back into Alice's voice, Nick continued. "I know I have subpoenas to serve around your neighborhood this week. I'll have a word with Geoff about taking my lunch break and drop by with a picnic or something."

A silence followed, then Nick heard her soft sigh. It was the best he could offer in the awkwardness of her last week in town, and he sent a quick prayer heavenward that she would appreciate the gesture.

"Nick. I think that is…" Alice's voice trailed off, and Nick pushed himself up to sit on the edge of the bed. His shift was starting soon, and he wanted to begin the night on a positive note. "Nick, I don't like the chances of it happening, but I love the idea."

Nick grinned to himself. If she didn't believe he could make it happen, it just made him more determined to make sure it did.

CHAPTER
TWENTY - EIGHT

Nick pulled up outside Alice's family home for the last time and his eyes travelled over the gardens and homestead. He could see through the windows that the house was now empty. Alice would be gone in just a couple of hours.

His mind recalled their last week. So many ideas of how they thought they'd spend it, but as the time drew on, things just didn't play out as planned. Even the proposed picnic idea fell through thanks to a high-speed chase through the city which ended with three underage drivers being arrested.

The front door opened and Alice stepped out, her eyes were downcast as she pulled the door closed behind her. Nick pushed their disastrous last week from his mind and watched the last look she gave the house before looking over at him: a mix of trepidation and elation. Fear of the unknown mingled with the thrill of new beginnings.

The passenger side door opened and she dropped into the seat next to him, filling his car with some spicy sweet scent that reminded him of Christmas eggnog and vanilla candles. "You, ok?"

Alice tossed her hair back and looked at him. "Yeah. It's going to be great." Her chin tipped as she laid her fingertips on his forearm. "I was actually just talking to my new boss. He's going to pick me up at the airport and take me to where I'll be working to meet some of the team and pick up my things ready to start work on Monday."

Nick felt his eyebrows jump as he checked his blind spot then pulled out onto the road. "Can't your parents do that?"

"They're going to meet the removalists at the new house…"

Nick glanced at Alice. She was all smiles as she looked out the front window and talked about the plans for when the family landed. Excitement had won over the earlier sadness in her expression and he chuckled.

"What's so funny?" Alice gave his arm a light slap. Nick took her hand and entwined her fingers in his. "I'm going to miss you."

The words came out before he could think, and a sudden lump appeared in his throat. He felt Alice's hand on the side of his cheek, and he glanced at her. "I will miss you too, Officer Marshall."

In what seemed like no time at all they arrived at the airport. Nick pulled up in the drop-off zone as the afternoon sun cast long shadows along the ground. He turned off the engine. Mr. and Mrs. Knight stood with Marcus and Sarah, waiting outside the terminal entrance. Luggage surrounded them and smiles as bright as Christmas trees lit their faces. Alice turned to him. "You wanna come in? You know, wave goodbye from the window?"

Nick laughed as he looked away. "It's not goodbye." He turned back to her. "I'll see you in three weeks for New Years. Our first anniversary."

Alice leaned in and linking her fingers behind Nick's neck, pressed a lingering kiss to his mouth. He cupped the back of her head, holding her in place. He couldn't imagine being without her for three weeks. It was going to test him. "I look forward to New Year's." Nick murmured against her lips.

Alice moved back from him slowly, letting her fingernails run along his neck before her fingers fell away. "Until New Year's then."

"Call me when you land." Nick watched as Alice collected her bag and slipped from his car. She gave a quick nod, blew him a kiss, closed the door and was soon lost in the flow of people.

She was gone.

A honk behind him geared Nick into action and he started up his car. Pulling out of the drop off zone, he turned towards home.

To get ready for work.

* * * *

The office was quiet when Nick entered for the graveyard shift. Taking his hat off and sliding it onto his desk, he waved hello to Geoff before continuing to the kitchen for a coffee.

With prayers for a quiet night, Nick put Alice and the fanciful thoughts of when he'd see her again at New Year's from his mind. He had to show Geoff he was 100% focused on the job. The man's opinion of his professionalism meant the world to him and his success as a police officer.

Coffee in hand and diary under his arm, Nick joined Geoff with the other graveyard shift officers in the meeting room for handover.

The day had been non-stop. Even before the outgoing crew spoke, Nick could see it on their faces – they were exhausted. A fatal overdose, a train station brawl that resulted in a number of people hospitalized, relocating a homeless man to a safer place to sleep... it had been full-on. He took notes and files, exchanged laughs and quips then headed back to his desk.

"Better get into the paperwork before the night hots up, kid." Geoff's voice sounded from over the cubical wall. Nick fired up his computer and the tapping of keyboard strokes filled the workspace. "On it, sir. Hope it's a quiet one."

"A quiet shift is a good shift." Geoff called back. "It means everyone's obeying the law."

Nick chuckled and reached for his phone. Unable to concentrate on anything until he knew Alice had safely landed, he wanted to check his messages first.

Nothing.

He checked the time. Her plane had departed over three hours ago, she should be there by now. He turned his pen end on end. Where was she?

Distracted, Nick opened his emails. Maybe she was just busy with family and new colleagues? He put the phone down. She'd message soon enough. Nick threw back the rest of his coffee as he worked through the emails: updated training dates for the New Year, OHS reminders, Christmas holiday roster changes... he paused.

What was this?

Nick replaced the now-empty coffee mug on his desk and reread the last email. The name mentioned was his, but the station was different and the wording in the body of the email didn't make sense. A typo?

The mobile phone on his desk vibrated and, forgetting the emails, Nick pounced on it. Anticipating to see a message from Alice, he punched in his pin and opened his phone. His sister's name flashed on the screen. Disappointment exited in a sigh and a humorless grin tugged at the corner of his mouth as he read Beth's message about a movie she was watching. His mind was still on Alice.

It was not like her to not make contact.

Lord be with her. Keep her safe. Please.

CHAPTER
TWENTY-NINE

The sounds of metal clanging echoed around the locker room, signaling the end of the graveyard shift. Nick waved off his colleagues as he moved at snail's pace. He couldn't get Alice off his mind.

Thoughts began to steal into his head about the security of their relationship, while the memory of Trent's words to him haunted him.

It's the Lord's time to be with her.

Though she had messaged early in the morning full of apologies, the doubts had crept in. The fact that she was already talking about new colleagues in a familiar way wasn't helping – one person in particular seemed to be getting more than his fair share of airtime. Sure, he was her training officer, so it was to be expected, but Nick's mind was still doing funny things.

Sleep was becoming more difficult; the dreams continued, paperwork was building.

He felt stressed and his body did not like night shifts.

Unfastening his load-bearing vest, Nick checked over his kit. The pepper spray needed replacing. Placing the container to the side, Nick continued to check over the items. Just then, movement across the room drew his attention. "Eddie. You're late."

Eddie opened the locker beside Nick and began to put his personal items in and take out his load-bearing vest. "It's going to be a long day."

"You'll be right. Just don't wake me up when you get home." Finished de-kitting, Nick gave Eddie a couple of hard raps on his back and hung up his load-bearing vest. Closing his locker, he moved out of the room.

Travel mug steaming in hand, Nick collected his phone and wallet from his desk and headed towards the exit. Just as he'd reached the rear door, Eddie appeared by his side. "Got a quick sec?"

Nick looked at his housemate with curiosity. His hushed voice and the worry behind his hazel eyes held his interest; a sprinkle of goosebumps ran up his arms. "Sure. Everything ok?"

Eddie stepped closer, "Not me, mate. You. Can we talk somewhere in private?"

Just as Nick gave a nod and gestured with his travel mug towards a meeting room, Eddie's senior officer appeared beside them. "Hastings, we leave in two. Good to see you, Nick. Enjoy some rest time."

"Yes, Sir." Nick exchanged a look with Eddie while worry nipped at his mind. What could have put the wind up his mate so much that they couldn't speak about it openly or wait until they were home? With a silent prayer for protection, Nick pushed out the door towards the car park.

*   *   *   *

"Ed?"

Nick entered the living room, stretching out his shoulders. He knew Eddie had returned home – announced by the bang of the front door. He'd asked Eddie not to wake him. The man just couldn't be quiet.

Peering out the window to the outdoor area, he caught sight of Eddie at the BBQ speaking on his mobile. Nick gave the glass a light tap and, when Eddie turned around, he waved, still wearing a scowl.

Last night's shift had been tough, Nick recalled, as he switched the kettle on. When he and Geoff had been called out to a welfare check they were diverted to an urgent incident – a traffic crash involving a truck and three cars. Dispatch had informed them there were people injured.

Nick ran a hand through his hair as a rush of the anxiety raced through his body once again. Closing his eyes, he began to form a prayer for calm when he heard the door open and looked up to see Eddie entering, bringing with him the smokey scents from the BBQ.

The man had a firm look about him as he approached the opposite side of the kitchen bench. Nick straightened, forgetting the earlier grip of anxiety over his last shift, and set his mind on what was bothering his house mate. "Afternoon, Ed."

"I think you might have a problem brewing."

"Over what?"

Eddie splayed his hands on the kitchen bench and leant on his arms. "I overheard some other officers talking this morning in the car park. That's why I was late. Mate, they were talking about you being an informant for the drug cartel that Jack was involved in."

Nick felt the blood drain from his face. He placed one hand on the bench and pocketed the other, trying to remain calm. "What?"

"Yeah. It's serious."

"They said my name?"

"Yes."

"Well what did you say?"

"I didn't roll down my car window and join in. Thought I'd get some intel first."

Nick ran both hands through his hair and held the back of his head. "What else did you hear?"

"Look, I know you're checking in with the detectives about the status of the case involving your friend's brother because you're keeping an eye out for your friends. But the other guys don't know that. What I heard is they think you're leaking information back to the cartel and that is why the detectives can't get near these guys."

There was a firmness in Eddie's expression which meant there was nothing more to add. Nick blew his breath out, dropped his arms and moved out of the kitchen to head to his room. "Who was talking?" He called back to Eddie.

"Adams and Black."

Nick looked at his watch. Detective Brooks would have knocked off already. He turned back to Eddie at the mouth of the hallway. "Well, first thing tomorrow I'll have to sort this out. Thanks for informing me."

The door closed behind Nick with a soft click. For a long moment Nick stood looking out his window at the late afternoon shadows moving over the backyard. Why would two colleagues be thinking these things? "They know I'm a close contact and I'm concerned about my friends and myself – well, who wouldn't be?" Nick mumbled to himself. Then, reaching for his phone he called Dylan. He picked up after the third ring. Laughter could be heard before he heard Dylan's greeting. "Nick, brother, how's it going?"

Unsure to start a heavy conversation hearing sounds of a party in the background, Nick rubbed the back of his head. "Having a party there, are you?"

A door closed, muffling the background noise coming down Dylan's line and Nick pictured him entering his bedroom. "Well, Mum's been a bit flat since Jack was taken into witness protection. Not knowing anything about how he was doing was starting to get her down. So, Lex suggested a little Christmas gathering for her. Uncle Shane is here and some of Lachlan's mates from the club. Lex and I are pretty much the hired help."

Nick smiled at the imagery Dylan's description painted in his mind. "I won't keep you. I just wanted to touch base. Nothing out of the ordinary been happening, has it?"

"No. It's all quiet."

"Good." Nick gave a firm nod of his head. He hadn't heard anything either, and with the stalker back behind bars there was nothing to alarm him. Detective Brooks told him if they uncovered anything that concerned him, he'd let him know. Surely if Brooks thought Nick was a leak, he'd say something!

"Everything ok?" Dylan's voice was a note lower and filled with concern. Nick blew his breath out, not wanting to say anything until he'd cleared things up at the station. "Yeah. All good. You two have a great night."

"You too, brother. See you at the Christmas Eve service."

"I'll be there. See you then."

CHAPTER THIRTY

"Just me again." Nick spoke to Alice's answering machine. "Thinking of you. Call me when you're free. Or message. Whatever. Missing you."

Nick tossed the phone onto his bed, pulled on his police shirt and, after tucking it in, fastened his belt. Where was Alice? It had been days since she'd returned a message and even longer since they'd spoken. She sounded ok when they spoke, though. He needed to talk to her, now more than ever – to hear her reassurance and encouragement that whatever was brewing at work would be ok. That would go a long way with helping him through the day.

As soon as he arrived at work, he was going to see Detective Brooks and try to sort out what Eddie had informed him of yesterday.

* * * *

"Detective Brooks." Nick rapped the back of his knuckles on the frosted glass pane of the office door. "Have you got a sec?"

A moment passed before the detective looked over at Nick from his computer and waved him in. "Come in. Have a seat."

Nick moved into the office and sat down, eager to have the weight on his chest removed after Eddie had saddled him with it last night. Sleep had been impossible. "Sir, I'd like to get right to the bottom of why I'm here."

Detective Brooks clasped his hands over his desk and gave Nick his full attention. "Do you have some information on the case we are working on?"

With a light shake of his head, Nick edged forward on his seat. "No. I am here because a fellow officer has told me that they heard colleagues talking about me being an informant to this cartel you are trying to catch. Have you heard about this?"

The look on the detective's face told Nick he did not know this was going on. He rose and moved at pace to the door of his office and closed it. "Who's talking?"

"Adams and Black, sir."

"And who informed you of this?" Detective Brooks moved back to his desk and scooped up his pen, resumed his seat and pulled a notepad out of his shirt pocket.

It was on Nick's tongue to say Eddie, but a flash through his mind that he should hold his silence caused him to pause. Detective Brooks looked up. "Marshall? Who told you of this?"

Nick shifted in his seat. "Sir?"

"Well, did you make it up, or is there someone I can have verify this allegation?"

The man's laser beam expression pierced through Nick's hesitation, and he gave in to the detective. "Officer Eddie Hastings, Sir. We are house mates. He told me he heard Adams and Black conversing in the car park before start of shift yesterday. He'd informed me of this last night when we got home."

Nick watched the detective's pen work furiously across the notepad while his mind formed a haphazard prayer that Eddie would be ok in all this, as he sensed something was off. The scratch of Detective Brooks' pen stopped, and he looked over the table at Nick. "Anything else you want to add?"

The walls of the detective's office began to feel like they were closing in under the man's hard stare. However, the memory of the strange email he had received came back to mind. Nick sat forward in his chair. "There was a strange email I received last week."

"Who was it from?"

A rap on the glass pane of the detective's office saw his intense gaze shift over Nick's head as he called for the visitor to come in. Nick turned as the door latch clicked, and he saw Geoff enter.

"Nick, we gotta hit the road. You finished, Wayne?"

Nick began to rise from his chair and looked at Detective Brooks to thank him for his time. The man was on his feet, hands on hips. "Send me that email as soon as you get back to your desk, before you head out with Geoff."

CHAPTER THIRTY-ONE

"Alice!" Nick said, surprised at hearing her voice on the other end of his phone. "Thought you'd gone under cover or something. Where have you been? They keeping you busy up North, eh?"

Thrilled that she had called, Nick slumped onto the couch and put his feet up on the chaise. "It's so good to hear your voice."

A soft chuckle came down the line, drawing his smile out the more. "Same to you, Nick. I can't stay on the phone for long, but I had to talk to you."

Sad to hear she had to go soon, but encouraged that she needed him, he resigned himself to another quick phone call. "That's ok. I understand our timetables are not working together very well at the moment. I'm looking forward to New Year's when I can come up to visit you."

"Yeah. About that…"

Nick felt his smile fall away and he pushed himself up.

"Nick. There's no easy way to say this, but I think we should see other people."

Though he'd been expecting that this was coming, it still hit him like a freight train. Unsure what to say, Nick held his silence, waiting to hear if Alice would say anything further. He heard her soft sigh and wondered if it was because she was sad or if she was wondering how much longer she had to stay on the phone before she could hang up. He sensed it was the latter.

"Nick? You there?"

Nick grunted. "Yeah."

"Do you want to say anything, or do we just hang up and that's it?"

"I guess I'm a little confused really. You said, when I came to talk to you about us before you left, that there was nothing we can't work through together. What's changed?"

"I guess I was wrong." Alice's reply was cool, and Nick felt his brow crease in thought. He had the urge to face this standing up. Pushing himself off the bed he crossed to his window and looked out at the early morning light streaming through the trees. He couldn't believe he was about to ask this next question. He dropped his head into his hands. "Are you seeing someone else?"

The silence that followed answered his question. He looked back up and out the window. The cheery sunlight mocked him, and he felt a snarl creep over his face. So many questions he wanted to ask, but what was the point?

"Nick?"

The soft way Alice said his name brought a lump to his throat. When this phone call ended, they would never speak again. A chasm was opening up within him and breath was becoming hard to draw in. "There's nothing to say. I understand what cheating is."

"Nick it's…"

"Alice, look. Don't bother. Merry Christmas." Nick pulled the phone from his ear and ended the call. He could hear her inaudible words before the line cut their connection, and he stood for a moment staring at the now blackened screen in his hand. They'd been together just under a year, though he'd planned for many more to come. Tossing his phone on the bed, he moved out to the living room, unsure of what to do next.

* * * *

"You hung up on her!"

Nick side-eyed Hope as he rubbed his temples, his body slumped over his knees. "I know. A real low moment."

The church was lit with candles and dimmed-down lights for the Christmas Eve service. Nick sat backstage with his friends, waiting for the first of the youths to arrive. They were to help them get ready for the songs they were going to sing, and play they were going to perform in the Christmas Eve service.

"Give him a break, Hope." Dylan jumped in, laying a few raps across Nick's back. "He'd just found out she'd been cheating on him. We all react differently to shocking news."

With a long sigh, Nick sat back and lay his limp arms in his lap. "Thanks, D."

"I can't believe it." Lexi said. Her voice came from far away as she dug around in the stage props, sounding like she was deep in thought. "I really liked Alice. Never would have guessed you guys would end this way – or at all really."

Nick slowly nodded. The week had dragged on. Somehow, he had managed to get through his shifts and paperwork and not call or message Alice. He felt numb – in a dream he wanted to wake up from only couldn't.

"Go home, we'll handle tonight." Dylan rose from beside him and went to Lexi, who was trying to reach something from the back of the props wardrobe. Nick turned to watch Trent atop a ladder fastening fairy lights along the top of the stage that Hope was handing up to him, and now that Dylan fishing things out for Lexi from the wardrobe he felt like a spare wheel.

"How are we all going in here?" Dave's voice rang out from the stairwell, moments before his face appeared. "Cars are rocking up. The kids will be here in just a moment."

A chorus of reports rang out from his friends as they updated Dave where they were up to, as the stampeding of feet could be heard in the hall. Nick pushed himself up, not wanting the young people to see his mood, and looked around for something to busy himself with. Noticing Hope trying to unknot a section of the lights, he went to see if he could lend a hand. As he approached, he picked up on the conversation she was having with Trent.

"I am just so excited!" Hope's head was down as she worked the wires. "I mean, I've heard about fly n build mission trips before I was a Professional Volunteer, but I never thought I'd be going on one. But now that I am, I'm more excited about this than Christmas!"

Nick chuckled and Hope glanced up at him, a warm smile welcomed him to the conversation as she turned back to the task her hands were working on.

She looked to be making the knot worse. Nick pocketed his hands. "Where is the trip too?"

"Papua New Guinea!" Hope paused in her efforts to unknot the lights and her shoulders relaxed as she looked up at Trent, then over to Nick again. "Can you believe it? Me, helping out on a fly and build mission trip!"

While sharing a chuckle with Hope, Nick surreptitiously slipped the knotted lights out of her hands. "I'm impressed Hope! When do you leave?"

"The day before New Years." Hope swung her now empty hands by her sides. The energy emanating from her was barely being contained. "We'll have a couple days to settle in before getting started on site." Nick handed the now unknotted lights up to Trent. "You given her any build site tips yet?"

A grin spread across Trent's mouth as he reached up to secure the last of the lights, his voice held a note of strain as he fiddled at the end of his reach with the light clips. "Yeah, a few basics."

"I have a list of things to organize before I head off." Hope chimed in, holding the ladder for Trent. "But I'll be mostly administration and outreach. I won't be using any building tools."

"How long will you be gone?"

"One month."

Nick gave a dip of his head just as Trent dropped down from the ladder he was standing on, closed it up and swung it out of the way. "What's Josh have to say about it?"

There was a slight dulling of her energy. "Oh, yeah, he is happy for me."

"A month is a long time." Trent rejoined them and Hope looked at him with a nod of her head.

"Yeah! I'm going to miss him."

Nick tried his best empathetic impression while listening to Hope, though the last thing he wanted at the moment, let alone on Christmas Eve, was to think about relationships. He didn't need any reminders about Alice and end up down a pity party wondering what she might be doing with her new boyfriend. He gave Hope a jab to her upper arm. "You'll be right. C'mon, let's get into the church."

CHAPTER THIRTY-TWO

Nick sat at the back of the church watching people file in and take their seats ready for the evening program. He was enjoying the feeling of peace that filled his mind as he gazed at the stage. Soft-glowing lamps lit up a manger scene, while fairy lights arranged in the shape of a star hung high above it. Surprised that the animal props looked as good as they did, Nick found himself smiling – he'd been against the animal prop idea, thinking it would look terrible, but the youths had pulled it off. He was so proud of them.

Unbidden, the conversation with Dave came back into his mind. What did God see in him? He didn't have enough time to work with the young people like Dave did, nor could he create engaging programs for the youths like Dave did. He didn't have the same energy as Dave or have a woman to back him up – not anymore. Nick dropped his head and toyed with his military style wristwatch. Why would God think he was appropriate to be the next leader?

"How good does the set look?" Dylan slipped into the seat next to him. Nick leaned over to see he was by himself. "Yeah, I'm impressed. Where's Lexi?"

"She and Hope are getting the supper finalized. How are you doing?"

Nick gave a snort of derision. "Great. Is that what you were expecting me to say?"

Dylan gave an shake of his head. "Nah, there's more to it. Since you were going to end things with her only a few weeks back, I find the funk you're in quite deep considering. Tell me, how's work going? How's your family? Are your sisters ok?"

"You wanna have a deep and meaningful conversation here?" Nick leaned towards his friend, keeping his voice low. "The church service is about to start."

"Then give me the short version." Dylan fired a wink at him and Nick turned back to face the stage, crossing his arms. The quick version? Ok. Turning to Dylan, he cleared his throat. "Well, you asked for it.… I'm either being stitched up at work, or there is some sort of miscommunication that has mixed me up with the crowd your brother was with. There's talk of me being an informant and that's why they can't catch these guys." Satisfied to see the surprise behind Dylan's eyes, Nick continued. "I'm still having anxiety about attending incidents as a first responder. I thought I had worked through it but after attending an incident a few weeks ago, it all came back and I'm booked in again with the counselor. Oh, and I got dumped by my cheating girlfriend over the phone just before Christmas."

A couple moved passed them with polite greetings and wishes for the season and, after a quick chat about the youth program for the year, continued moving towards where some empty seats in the fast-filling church.

Nick took a drink from his bottle while he waited for Dylan to work out his response, as evident by the ever-changing expressions across his face. He recapped his bottle and glanced towards the front of the church. Trent was in place with the stage band, and they were getting their music sorted on the music stands.

"Nick, mate, this is serious. What are they doing about the allegations?"

'O Holy Night' began floating through the air as the band began playing. Nick watched the musicians a moment longer before turning back to Dylan. His voice hushed. "They're looking into it. The detective does not for a moment believe I have anything to do with it, so he's looking into where the gossip started. It's just unsettling, I guess you could say. And distracting."

"Look out to those who try to get you in trouble." Dylan's voice held such a confident note of authority, Nick found a smile creep upon his face – which Dylan mirrored. "Hey there he is. We lost you for a moment. Welcome back."

Nick chuckled and looked back to the musicians. "Thanks, mate."

Silence passed between them while 'O Holy Night' seamlessly blended into 'Away in a Manger'. The atmosphere was so peaceful and reverent Nick did not wish to be anywhere else.

It was Christmas!

A time to reflect on what an incredible act of love Jesus did to save us. He would not waste the opportunity to share Jesus with those around him, because of things happening his in personal life. God knows what He is doing – no matter how much it hurts.

CHAPTER
THIRTY-THREE

*C*hristmas came and went in a blur. While all around was an atmosphere of celebration with fairy lights, street decorations and town carols, there were also the holiday irresponsible drivers that were threatening to swallow Nick up each time the CB radio crackled into life.

On the morning of New Year's Eve, Nick strode out to his car to head into work, a heaviness forming in his gut. Was it because it was a year ago he and Alice had become a couple and now she was gone? Or was it because there was going to be an even higher chance of incidents out on the road? *Lord, help me. I feel like I'm drowning.*

As soon as Nick entered the station his worries were confirmed. Extra staff swarmed around the office while an almost constant ring of telephones trilled throughout the building. Nick greeted his fellow officers as he made his way to the muster room.

"Worried about something, Marshall?"

Nick slipped into one of the plastic seats opposite Geoff and placed his travel mug on the table. "Why do you say that, sir?"

"Your knuckles are white on that travel mug at eight in the morning. Any man worth his salt can see something's put the wind up you."

Before Nick could string a sentence together to answer his shrewd senior officer, Detective Wayne Brooks and Inspector Colin Hartford entered the room. Nick leaned forward, curious to know what the two men were going to report to the room.

"Good morning officers." Inspector Hartford said, while organizing his notes on the podium in front of him. "A few important announcements before you head out. Officers Adams and Black have been stood down impending investigation into claims they've been spreading rumors about other officers. Moreover, our stalker friend who broke his bail a few months ago has been sentenced and will be moved to the city corrections facility first thing this morning." Inspector Hartford stepped to the side and signaled for Detective Brooks to step up to the podium.

"Thanks, Colin." Brooks said before clearing his throat. "Listen up. You all know the drug cartel we have been following? Well, we have had a tip-off that there is a deal going down at some point this evening. We have our detectives and an undercover team going in, but just be aware out there. Screen your calls, do your checks and watch your backs."

Nick watched the two men leave the room without further word, while an undeniable sense of warning wove its tentacles through his mind. He reached for his coffee and listened to the hushed conversations around him. Unable to pinpoint why he was feeling keyed up, Nick sipped his drink and started to offer a prayer for protection when he felt Geoff's hand on his shoulder. He looked up. "Let's go, Nick. We've got a big day ahead."

* * * *

The freeway moved at snail's pace – both sides were full of backed-up cars. Nick was going over the paperwork on his lap once again, when he heard Geoff chuckle. He looked over at him. "What'd I miss?"

Geoff gave another light chuckle. "What's got your goat today. I've never seen you so edgy."

Unsure how to answer, Nick chuckled in reply. "Anxious to hear how the fellas go at the bust at some stage this evening. I'll sleep a lot better knowing that crowd have been caught and are behind bars."

The radio nattered away between them, the DJ speaking in excited tones about things happening around the city for New Year's Eve celebrations. It was irritating Nick's tightened nerves, and he leant forward to switch it off.

"No plans for tonight, I guess?" Geoff chuckled again as he took a left into a quiet side street. Nick looked out the window at the passing houses. The sun was shimmering through the canopy trees and kids on school holidays were riding bikes and scooters down the footpaths. Bright smiles lit their faces, revealing not a worry in their minds. "It's the next house here on the right, Geoff." Nick gestured across the car, forcing his mind back on the job."

The light tick of an indicator sounded, and Geoff steered the car into the driveway that Nick had pointed out.

Approaching the door alongside Geoff, Nick found himself hyper aware of his surroundings. He looked to his left and right. A bird chirped; he looked up. Kids called to each other, and he looked behind them.

"Get a hold of yourself Marshall. You lead."

Nick squared his shoulders and climbed the front porch steps, then rapped on the door a loud three knocks. Geoff was right, he had to focus back on the job. *Jesus help me...*

An imposing Caucasian man opened the door and stepped into Nick's space. Nick held the man's icy-blue stare and cleared his throat. "Are you Mr. Saul McGuire, birthdate April 6 1968?"

The man continued his hard stare. Nick coached himself to not break eye contact and to give a few moments before repeating his question, while his mind recalled details of what this guy had done in order to have a court summons handed to him.

Just then Saul glanced at Geoff, and Nick found the opening to repeat his question. The silence from Saul continued and Nick held up a photograph of the man. "Mr. McGuire you have been identified via this photograph and we are here to serve you these documents." A snarl began to crawl along Saul's mouth. A chill ran up Nick's spine, though his hand remained steady as he held out the documents. He knew Geoff was silent beside him in order to examine Nick's performance, and he was determined to do well. Deciding the man wasn't going to speak or take the documents off him, Nick bent to leave the papers at Saul's feet. Rising, he gave a brief nod then turned. His mind whirled with the possibilities of what might happen, causing his palms to start sweating.

Once back at the car, Nick clicked his buckle into place then looked back at the front door. Saul was still staring at him with a look that went beyond internal anger. The car started. Nick felt the vehicle moving backwards but he couldn't tear his eyes away. If he didn't know better, he'd say that look was one of recognition and restraint.

A threat.

Nick's blood ran cold.

CHAPTER THIRTY-FOUR

*S*uspicion began to gnaw at Nick. He'd woken up with an odd feeling this morning, and that wasn't helping. Why did the perpetrator glare at him so…hungrily?

"Good job back there. He was a tough one."

Nick looked at Geoff. He was relaxed in his seat, arm resting on the door while he held the steering wheel. Did he not sense it? Bypassing the compliment from his superior, Nick angled himself towards Geoff. "Sir, did you not think there was something up with that guy?"

"What do you mean?" Geoff moved the car around a slow-moving truck. "People don't tend to roll out the welcome mat when getting served."

"D24 to Mount Vale 375."

Nick swallowed his reply to Geoff as the man picked up the handpiece. "375 receive. Go ahead."

"Code 10 in your area."

Nick felt relief flood his body that the call was for a Domestic Dispute and not a traffic incident. As Geoff relayed back that they would take the call, Nick pulled the job details up on the iPad and put Saul from his mind. With prayers for calm in his mind, Nick sat back in his seat as Geoff switched on the lights and sirens then set the car off towards the listed address.

The street was unusually quiet for New Year's Eve, Nick thought as Geoff turned the patrol car into an area of the city he'd not been to before. He checked the notes he'd taken down from dispatch. "House number 56."

"56. Got it. Radio in, code 5. We've arrived."

"Everything alright?" Nick asked. The car door cracked open as Geoff moved to exit their vehicle. There was a different air about him – his movements were stiffer. Nick cracked open his door and slipped out.

Geoff gestured for him to hurry up and, once they were together, moved off silently towards the front door. "It's too quiet for a D.D."

Nick felt the hairs on the back of his neck rise as he fell into step behind Geoff.

The veranda was littered with flowering potted plants and a budgie singing in a cage, but in Nick's mind there was a dark shadow about the place. As he looked back towards the street, he heard the hard knocks Geoff laid on the front door. ae turned back to see who would answer. It was too quiet.

No one responded and Nick watched as Geoff drew his weapon. He gave Nick a look that said he should do the same. An odd lightness of mind swept over Nick as he pulled out his gun – he'd never used it since being out of the Academy. The door gave easily when Geoff turned the handle and let himself in.

The house was quiet, and everything appeared to be in order. Nick's instincts kicked into overdrive as adrenalin began to fire throughout his body, tensing his muscles and sharpening his awareness. His footfalls were light as he followed Geoff through the sunlit living room and into the open dining and kitchen area.

A click drew his attention, and he turned towards the kitchen. Through the eyepiece he surveyed the vintage brown tile back splash and cream laminate benchtops... to find the kettle still steaming. Someone must be here. He glanced at Geoff. Geoff gestured with his head towards the front door. Nick slipped in behind Geoff and began taking slow steps backwards, keeping his gun raised towards the kitchen.

Just then a horn honked outside, breaking the silence. Nick glanced over his shoulder. The moment he did, he knew it was the wrong move. What sounded like a nail gun punched through the silence of the house and he turned back in time to see Geoff drop in front of him. Nick stared at the his superior slumped on the floor – a bright red syrup leaching out from under the side of his head.

Black, worn-looking steel-capped boots came into view beside Geoff's head. Just as Nick began to raise his eyes, another figure materialized in his peripheral.

Dread curled deep within his gut as he continued to lift his eyes to see who'd lured them to this place. Suddenly, a blinding light filled his vision and he felt himself stumble... the room went black.

CHAPTER THIRTY-FIVE

A sharp pain pulsated behind Nick's eyes in heavy thumps, growing in intensity until he felt himself drawn out of what felt like a deep sleep. Groggy, he tried to lift his arm to massage his temples but he couldn't move. Awareness began to dawn, and he struggled to peel his eyelids open to see where he was.

Trying to focus, Nick blinked his eyes a number of times until the double-vision merged into one picture. Panic rose in his chest as he tugged at his arm bonds, all the while letting his eyes travel around the empty warehouse that he was in. By the rich tangerine glow outside the derelict windows, he knew it was late afternoon. Where was he? Suppressing the fear that was threatening to take over, Nick turned his head as far as he could to each side, he needed to find something to identify his location. The steely tin walls were grey apart for some rust damage, and the concrete floor was clear of any type of stains – so he couldn't place what type of shed he was in. There was a slight smell of… wool? Nick screwed up his nose. Was he outside the city?

A roller-door opened, breaking into the quiet, and Nick hung his head again as if he was still unconscious. Maybe he could pick up something by listening to whoever had just entered? Heart pounding, Nick prayed fervently for help, while trying to keep his breathing even. He had to stall them somehow, or he was in serious trouble.

The conversation was hushed but for exaggerated swear words. They were agitated. Not good. Their footfalls were growing louder, and he knew they were making their way towards him. A scent of chicken began to fill Nick's nostrils and his stomach cramped. Was it from hunger or the sense of impending doom?

"He's still out? How hard did you hit him, Dan?"

The voice was gravelly; older. A smoker?

"Oh I don't know, Saul, I just hit him as you told me to. Maybe he's just weak?"

Saul? Nick's heart jumped into his throat. That wouldn't be a coincidence. Dan was answering through mouthfuls of the chicken he could smell. He sounded young.

"Can't you give him something to wake him up?"The younger guy said. There was a sound of hands rubbing as if he was dusting crumbs off his fingers.

"I say we give him ten minutes, then we start. He'll wake up then – I guarantee it."

The blood drained from Nick's head as laughter filled the room. Who were these guys and what did they want from him? His breathing was getting harder to control and he felt a shuddering in his body as adrenaline was trying to fight through the panic he was suppressing. Hands tied behind his back, and ankles tied to the wooden chair, there was nothing he could do. *God help me!* Nick cried out in his mind.

Just then a door slammed shut and echoed around the shed, followed by the sound of leather-soled shoes striding towards them. "What is going on here? Haven't you got started yet?"

"He's still out."

"Well, wake him up. The police will be all over us soon as they have no doubt discovered by now that the other cop's dead."

Nick's breath caught. Geoff was dead?

A new scent filled his nostrils. Cologne? The leather- soled shoes clapped the concrete floor towards him and Nick sensed whoever the new person was, he had stopped behind him. Instinctively, his muscles tensed.

The chair jerked back and Nick's eyes flew open. A well-dressed man with sunglasses looked back at him, his cruel mouth framed by a tidy goatee. "Nick Marshall. Nice of you to join us."

Pushed back onto four legs, the chair wobbled as Nick took in the two other men in the room. Suddenly, he was cuffed over the head. Grimacing as the pounding in his head rose in intensity, Nick lowered his eyes.

"Morons. How long has he been listening to you two?"

The polished shoes again clapped on the concrete and appeared in Nick's vision, while the other men remained silent. "So, Nick. How long have you been listening?"

Every fiber within his body told him to answer, but fear was tightening around his throat and drawing breath was an effort. He could sense an evil around him and his faith felt so tiny in comparison.

Smooth, cool fingers grasped his chin and tilted his head back. "I don't like to repeat myself."

"I didn't hear anything." Nick's words were strangled against the fight for breath. The man let go of his chin and crossed his arms. "I am sure you know why you're here. So, to save yourself, literally, just tell us what we want to know."

Nick glanced at the two other men then back at the suited man and gave a light shake of his head. It felt like it was going to crack open, and he needed a drink of water. "I don't know what you're talking about."

Saul cracked his knuckles and Nick looked at him again. The man reminded him of a caged dog just waiting for the gate to open.

"We know you're a friend of Dylan Saunders. We are looking for Jack but, alas, he's gone missing. Tell us where he is."

Nick tried a chuckle. "I'm a Police Officer, yes, but I only have limited access to information – particularly in regard to the witness protection program. You'd have had more luck with Geoff and shot me instead."

The suited man grinned as he drew a pistol and held it to Nick's head. Nick cringed and closed his eyes. "I don't believe you. You're best mates with Jack's brother. We've been watching you. Now, Jack owes us a lot of money and we want it back. So, you tell us where to find him, or things might not go so well for you tonight."

"I don't know anything, fellas." Nick tried to keep calm, but he heard the waver in his voice. Whatever they wanted to do, there would be no way of stopping them. His muscles began to twitch as an intense awareness of his vulnerability set in. '*God help me!*'

A click sounded and Nick felt his stomach bottom out knowing that the safety on the pistol had been released. "Surely you know something?"

Nick gave a rapid shake of his head. The suited man hummed, and Nick tried to control the pace his breathing was coming at. The thoughts in his mind raced though, and a cold sweat broke out over his face. He had seen who they were, there was no way they were going to let him go now.

Suddenly, the chair tipped on its side. The jarring action whipped Nick's neck, moments before his shoulder smashed into the cold concrete. Then followed his head – a dull thud that left the room spinning. Nick blinked. Once, twice. Feet moved towards him. The chair was kicked again, and Nick growled through clenched teeth at the deep ache that pulsated through his shoulder and rolled throughout his upper body.

"Send Mick after the girl since that last idiot got busted again. And the brother, send Big Daz after him. I want Jack found. Tonight!"

Nick blinked again. Willing his sight to clear, he watched the polished shoes disappear while a sick dread began to swirl in his stomach. Lexi! Dylan!

"What do we do with him?" Saul's dark voice invaded the chilling thoughts of his friends.

"Do what you want with him. He's useless to us."

A heavy door closed, heightening Nick's terror, just as the chair Nick was on was flipped onto its back. Nick cried out as a foot rested on the seat, crushing his arms that were still tied behind the chair and further grinding the damage to his shoulder socket. Saul stood over him and grinned a snarl that revealed missing teeth. Nick forced his mind to record any detail in case he made it out of here alive.

"Dan. Bring it over." Saul leaned his weight further over the chair and Nick sucked in his breath. "I think you'll like this."

Nick turned his head from the evil shining in Sauls' eyes to the movement he saw to his right. Dan was loping towards them, a syringe in his hand.

Nick furiously struggled against the weight over him and the ties that bound him. Dan handed Saul the syringe and Nick turned his wide eyes back to Saul. Saul took the cap off the needle with his yellowed teeth and positioned the syringe towards Nick's thigh. "They say, never knock something before you've tried it. Well, I'm sure we'll be seeing you again after this – maybe you can pay back the money you've cost us. If you survive, that is."

"No!" Nick pulled against the ropes, as Saul and Dan shared a chilling laugh. The pain in his shoulder and head dulled by adrenaline, he wriggled as much as he could in hopes of messing up the target Saul was aiming for.

"Oh, will you do something?!" A string of foul language combined with spittle sprayed from Saul's mouth as he gripped Nick's thigh with his steel-like fingers.

"What do you want me to do?" Dan's voice was like a frightened bird as he stood, fidgeting beside Nick.

"I don't care! Something!"

Nick's eyes glimpsed the dirty white running shoe coming towards him moments before he felt his head jerked back. Once, twice. His vision blurred and the room slipped from view.

CHAPTER THIRTY-SIX

Unintelligible shrieks broke into Nick's conscious, followed by excruciating pain radiating through his body. Still laying on his arms on the over-turned chair, he winced as more shouts rang out. His head was thumping but, intrigued by the fear in those screams Nick inched his head to the side to look towards them.

He managed to peel an eye open just enough to make out the three men backed up against the rear wall of the warehouse. His vision blurred again, and he tried a couple of blinks. A flash of intense light speared the room, so bright he couldn't look. He turned his head away, then grimaced as pain laced his body.

The sound of wind swept past him and, blinking, Nick turned his head in the direction it went. An intimidating figure now stood before the men, who cowered like beaten dogs. Goosebumps raised over Nick's arms and he couldn't tear his eyes away. As he looked on, the backlit figure turned and looked right at him. The eyes were luminous and bore into Nick's, surprisingly filling him with a sense of peace and wonder. Darkness crept into the edges of his vision once again, and everything went black.

* * * *

"Suspected acromioclavicular or clavicular fracture of the left shoulder. Numerous contusions across the Occipital to Sphenoid, lacerations to wrists and ankles. Tachycardic, dilated pupils, cold extremities."

Nick moaned as he rolled his head back and forth over the soft mound behind his head. Much nicer than the concrete floor. Was he dreaming? Who was the female speaking? Were his friends ok?

Warm fingertips lay across his forehead. "Officer Marshall, my name is Beth Doran. I am a paramedic. You're in the ambulance. You're safe. It's important you remain still." Nick felt the fingertips close around his hand. "Can you tell me your name? Squeeze my hand if you understand what I'm saying."

How did he get into the ambulance?

A memory of luminous eyes filled his mind and he recoiled, drawing his breath in tightly.

"Officer Marshall, you're ok. You need to stay still for me. Can you squeeze my hand?"

The female voice was closer. An irritating beep nearby was increasing in speed, it's pitchy sound felt like water torture within his mind. He rolled his head over the pillow.

The faces of the men as they cowered before the figure in the warehouse raced through his mind. The wind that had rushed past him. The flash of light like the sun. The eyes as the figure turned to look at him.

Darkness was closing in again. He could hear the paramedics talking to each other. Nick tried to open his eyes. He tried to speak but a garbled moan filled his ears. Straps across his chest and legs restricted his attempt to sit up until he felt a hand on his shoulder. "Nick, I need you to lay back. Try to rest. You're ok. Take deep breaths for me. In, out. In, out."

A pillow once again cradled the back of his head and he felt the darkness creeping up on him again. He no longer resisted, and fell into its grasp.

* * * *

Nick groaned as he, yet again, tried to open his eyes. His mouth felt like a dry, sandy desert and he peeled his tongue off the roof of his mouth to lick his parched lips. He tried to roll his head over the pillow behind him. He wasn't moving, and there was a different smell in the air: air-conditioned air? Bleach?

"Oh, honey. Honey, he's awake."

A familiar scent enveloped him, and Nick cracked an eye open just enough to see his mum before him, and his dad right behind her. "Mum." His voice came out like a rasp, and he tried to clear his throat. He needed water.

"Shhh." Mrs. Marshall stroked the hair back from Nick's forehead. "Your father and I are here. Beth and Lauren are on their way. No need to talk. Just rest."

How did he get to the hospital? He frowned and tested his arms and legs. Dull aches greeted him but only his left arm was restricted in its movement.

A door opened and Nick heard someone with an authoritative voice address his parents in a hushed tone. Guessing it was the doctor, he turned his head towards the conversation and peered through the slit of his half-open eye. After a brief talk, the doctor moved towards the bed. "You are one lucky young man. How are you feeling?"

"My head is fuzzy." Nick tried to clear the rasp from his voice when he felt a straw press against his lips.

"Water, honey. Have a drink." The hushed voice of his mum instructed.

"That will fade." The doctor's rich, European accent spoke into the quiet of the room. "We have x-rayed your left shoulder and confirmed the paramedics' suspicions. You've sustained an acromioclavicular fracture which will need to be immobilized for four to six weeks. We'll send you home with a physiotherapy schedule and follow-up appointments. Regarding the number of contusions to your head, you fortunately only have sustained a mild concussion. We will hold you here for 48 hours so we can monitor you, then we would like you to go home as long as someone remains with you at all times."

Nick felt his mum's grip around his hand tighten. "He'll come home with us, Doctor. His father and I will look after him."

A heaviness began to seep into his limbs as he listened to the conversation around him. He closed his eyes, shutting out the light and the concerned expressions marking the faces around his bed. What had happened felt like he'd watched a terrible B-grade movie, but the aches within his body told him otherwise. The heartrate monitor began to beep faster, and he heard the doctor request everyone leave the room to let him rest. Moments later he heard a nurse enter before he slipped into sleep's deep hold.

CHAPTER
THIRTY-SEVEN

he darkness was palpable, pressing in against his skin, drawing the breath from his body. Eyes. Luminous, chartreuse-green eyes, pinned him with such intensity that he couldn't look away. Closer and closer they drew, growing bigger and brighter as the distance between them diminished.

A sudden whoosh shattered the silence as looming shadows emerged behind those eyes, drawing his gaze up. Nick squinted as he tried to make out what the shimmering, glistening, silken-appearing objects were that rippled in a breeze that fluttered over his face. His gaze dropped to the eyes. They were right before him. Nick recoiled and cried out.

Nick's eyes flew open and, panting, he tried to push himself up on the bed and look around.

"Morning, son." Dave's voice rang out. "I was wondering when you were going to come around. I opened the curtains hoping the morning sun would rouse you."

Nick swallowed hard as he watched Dave move from the open window to the seat beside his bed. The smile from Dave's face faded, and he leant forward. "Take it easy, Nick. You're ok. It's January the second. Just lay back and try to rest."

"I, was, dreaming?" Nick looked around the white, sterile room while drawing deep breaths and letting them go in quick puffs. "It was intense." Nick looked back at Dave and touched a finger to his lip. Feeling a sizable gash, Nick withdrew his finger – checking for blood as memories of a dirty white running shoe filled his mind. "January second? Where did January first go? When did you come in?"

"The nurses told me you slept most of yesterday and that the doctors have you on strong painkillers. That might explain the intensity of the dream you were just having. They were about to come in with your breakfast, I offered to do it for them and opened the curtain to let some sun in."

Nick frowned, then touched his forehead. Something felt tight when he frowned. The curtain opening, the sun coming in, the open window – all fed into elements of his dream. At least that made sense. The rest, though…

"What were you dreaming about?"

Nick looked at Dave as he lowered his hand. The tone in his voice was more than just enquiring. "I'm not sure how to explain. It's disappearing fast."

An almost impassable lump formed in Nick's throat, and he reached with effort for his glass of water. What must he look like? An uncomfortable tug to his lip greeted the glass and he grimaced. He didn't want to know.

The door latch clicked and Nick looked over to see Lexi's head poking in, her smile tentative and voice just above a whisper. "Up for a few visitors?"

Lexi.

The last memory of her flashed through his mind. Conversation with Dave pushed aside to continue another day, he gave a weak grin. "Are you ok? Hope? Dylan?"

Lexi stepped into the room as a peaceable smile lit her features. "Yes. We are ok. Hope left the day before New Year's on a mission trip."

An overwhelming sense of relief filled his mind as he watched his friends enter the room. Dylan thumbed a gesture over his shoulder. "There are media crew everywhere outside. Police are stationed at your door."

Aware that his head was starting to let him know it was time to rest, Nick gave a weak lift of his eyebrows to Dylan's comment as he laid back against the pillows. "I'm not surprised. I'm sure they intended to kill me too."

A tangible silence fell over the room and Nick lowered his head. His eyes felt hot, and the onslaught of memories was making him nauseous. Movement in the room drew his attention back up and he narrowed his eyes as he watched Trent. The man closed the door before crossing the room. Nick could hear Lexi speaking, and in his peripheral saw Dylan sit on the edge of his bed, but it was Trent who held his focus. His green eyes were locked on Nick's as he lowered himself into a seat by the window.

Vivid memories flashed back through Nick's mind. The eyes… the shape of the shoulders… the hair. A sprinkle of goosebumps raised over his arms, and he started to push himself up again. "You." Nick's voice rasped, and he cleared his throat. "I mean, where were you when this happened to me?"

A timid giggle came from the area of the room Nick knew Lexi was sitting, but he didn't take his gaze off Trent. Honing everything he'd learnt; he watched the man like a hawk would watch for movement in a wheat field.

"What's going on?" Dylan's voice held the same tone Nick had picked up when he was coming to the end of his tether with

Jack – no nonsense. Nick held his hand up, while shooting Trent a questioning look. "You're the one who called the ambulance aren't you?"

Trent gave a shake of his head and Nick felt his breath rush out as he dropped his gaze. His head was fuzzy, but he knew he'd be dead if it wasn't for whoever called that ambulance. It had to be Trent.

He looked back at Trent. "Was Hope right about you?"

Dylan rose from the bed and faced Trent, while Lexi stepped closer to Nick's side. He felt her hand upon his shoulder and glanced at her. Her attention was aimed at Trent. "Trent, are you ok? I feel like Dylan and I have missed something."

Nick felt his breath rush out and he closed his eyes as a sudden dizziness enveloped him. He could hear Trent's soft voice as he spoke with Dylan and Lexi, but he couldn't grab what was said.

His room door opened, and he looked to see a nurse enter and approach the bed. She checked the clipboard, his drip, the sling, and heart monitor.

Tiredness pulled at him, and he felt his eyes close as his head dropped. The nurse lowered his bed back to prone position while asking everyone to leave the room. He didn't want them to go; he wanted his questions answered.

The sensation of sleep was approaching. Its warm embrace started to take over his mind and lure him away, although one thought hovered in his subconscious.

Trent is an angel?

CHAPTER THIRTY-EIGHT

Nick stepped over the threshold of his family's home and dropped the plastic hospital bag just inside the door. Home again.

"Can I get you anything?" Mrs. Marshall asked as she stepped around him, picking the bag up as she went.

It felt like it had been longer than four months since he'd lived at home, but at the same time like he'd only just left. Taking a few steps towards the living room, Nick lowered himself into the leather recliner and shook his head at his mum who was now looking at him over the kitchen bench.

A message sounded, and Nick dug his phone out of his pocket. Hope's name was on the screen, and he felt a lightness spread across his features, like an embedded frown had finally lifted. He opened the message.

'I know you've not been up to replying to messages, so just letting you know I'm thinking of you and things up here are going well... really well. LOL! See you when I get back. Stay safe, please.'

"You comfortable, honey?" Mrs. Marshall's voice cut into Nick's thoughts about finally replying to the mountain of text messages he'd received since his ordeal. He looked up to see his mum placing a sandwich and drink on the coffee table in front of him. Before he could say thank you, the doorbell rang and his mum went to the door.

Finger over his phone, Nick was just starting to answer Hope's messages when a familiar voice sounded in the room, and he looked over his shoulder.

Detective Wayne Brooks and Inspector Colin Hartford were passing his mum and making their way towards him. He went to stand, and the officers waved him down.

"Nick. Good to see you." Detective Brooks said as he removed his hat and lowered himself onto the lounge suite. "We tried a number of times to check in with you while you were in hospital, but every time we poked our head in you were asleep."

Inspector Hartford remained standing, his keen eyes drifting over Nick's face. "How are you doing?"

"All things considered, I think I'm doing quite well." Nick answered. He knew he wasn't a picture to look at, with half his face covered in shades of blues and purples and a sizable scab on his lower lip, but at least the swelling of his lower lip was going down. He picked up the drink his mum had left. "Can I get you anything?" Nick went to take a drink then sniffed in deprecation. "Or I could ask Mum to get you something?"

Light chuckles from his senior officers drew a reluctant grin from Nick before he sipped at the warm syrupy cappuccino. "Now, Nick." Detective Brooks said, his voice low. "We know you've been through quite an ordeal, and we can do this another time if need be..."

Nick replaced his drink on the coffee table and gave a shake of his head. "Thank you, sir, but I'll be ok. I'm eager to hear what happened while I was in hospital." The two officers exchanged a look which sent a warning zip up Nick's spine. He swallowed hard and trained his gaze on the detective.

"There's no easy way to say this, but Geoff has been killed in the line of duty."

Nick gave a firm nod of his head. "Yes, sir. I was aware. He went down in front of me…"

A sudden coldness swept over Nick's body and he reached for his drink… the room seemed to pull out, darkening at the edges. Blinking rapidly, he grasped his drink, only to notice the shake in his hands matched the trembling he felt deep within his muscles. Memories of what he'd seen flashed through his mind at an uncontrollable rate – the sound of the shot, the thud of Geoff hitting the ground…the color of blood that pooled from under his head. The shake in his hands intensified. Caramel-colored liquid slushed over the edges of the ceramic mug and over the coffee table.

Detective Brooks was beside him just as Nick realized he couldn't draw breath. Grabbing at the detective, Nick tried to get out what he was feeling but words would not come. He felt himself being moved from the edge of the recliner and laid out on the floor as a pillow was stuffed in behind his head. Somewhere in the room he could hear a shrill cry before a deep resonating voice silenced it.

"Nick. Look at me." Detective Brooks said, his voice commanding. Nick forced his unblinking eyes over to the detective's and he locked on them. He felt Brooks' firm grip on his hand. "Nick. You're having a panic attack. You are ok. Just lay still until it passes which won't be long – five to ten minutes. We'll be here the whole time."

Paralyzed with fear, as if he was back at the scene staring at Geoff's body and that pair of boots came into his view, Nick clung to the calm radiating from the detective's eyes. After what seemed like eternity, Nick felt his breath coming easier and his heart rate slow.

At his nod, the men eased Nick up into a seated position and sat near him. "I think we will do this another day. We've rung the ambulance and they'll be here within minutes."

At that moment, Nick heard the front door open, and he looked over his shoulder as two paramedics entered and were by his side before he could greet them. While they assessed him, Nick listened to Detective Brooks talk about how the drug cartel were caught, as well as the three men who had ambushed himself and Geoff. They also told Nick about the interviews that would be required of him for the investigation surrounding Geoff's death.

Nick leaned back against the lounge suite. It was a lot to take in, but a serene peace began to weave its way through the noise and settle his mind. Jack would be ok. Dylan's family would be safe. Geoff's death wasn't in vain. Realizing how close he had held onto this case and how much stress he had taken onto himself, the idea that he could let it all go now brought a swelling thankfulness to God.

CHAPTER THIRTY-NINE

The funeral of Geoff Eldridge had been hard. A lot harder than Nick had considered it would be. The mixed emotions of being back at the Academy and seeing fellow graduates, and farewelling a partner.

The lengthy police funeral procession and full police escort. The march behind the hearse along with hundreds of uniformed police officers' colleagues, while the mounted police unit followed. The countless members of the public that flowed back from the roads, along nature strips and far back on to the Academy lawns. It was more than he could bear.

Nick pulled on a shirt with difficulty. He felt numb. The faces of comrades and the general public as they looked upon him with eyes full of concern replayed in his mind, while their words of condolences and empty-sounding clichés echoed in his memories.

Geoff was dead?

A muscle in Nick's jaw clenched as he worked on the buttons of his shirt. He didn't want to go out, but he feared the depths his mind might sink to if he didn't. The evening was warm, his friends were waiting for him, and he was alive.

Though the meeting with Dave was not one the team were looking forward to, they all knew it had the happen. The date of Dave's departure was coming up fast and he wanted to start going through his office. Nick watched his reflection in the bathroom mirror as he buttoned his shirt one-handed. He didn't want to help clean out Dave's office. He didn't want Dave to leave them.

A knock on the front door drew him from his thoughts a moment before he heard his mum's voice echo through the house. "Nick, honey, I'm here. I'll wait for you in the car." Deciding that mum could do the last three buttons up, Nick readjusted the sling on his left arm, pocketed his phone and made his way out to the car where his mum was waiting.

All was silent as Nick stepped onto the open timber floor of the church hall. The stage was quiet, with its velvet red curtains swept to the side revealing their relaxing couches. The kitchen servery was open but there was no one in there.

He moved further into the room, his mind going over the years he'd spent attending this church and countless youth nights as a teen and now as a leader. His sandals slapped upon the floor as his eyes travelled every inch of the room. Suddenly a door banged open and he spun around with a start.

"Hey Nick, you made it!" Lexi's sing-song voice echoed through the hall as she passed Dylan holding the door open for her, her arms laden with books. "You're looking good!"

The pounding of his heart almost drowned out the cheerful greeting and Nick swallowed hard, trying to mask the fear response that was making its way through his body. He gave his right hand a shake before plunging it into his shorts pocket. "The clean-up has started already, has it?"

Lexi placed the books on the kitchen servery then turned back to him. "Oh, we just started. Dave had these books aside already for me. He thought I might find them useful if I go down the counseling pathway."

"You up for tonight?" Dylan asked, moving towards him. Nick met the steady look his friend gave him and with a slow nod of his head forced a grin. "Yeah."

"Did you want to check out some of Dave's books or want a cuppa first?" Lexi called over her shoulder as she entered the kitchen. "Definitely some books I saw in there that would be of use to you as a policeman."

Nick gave a distracted nod of his head. His days recovering had been filled with a haze of insecurity – could he go back to the force or not? Was Dave right? Was this career for him or was it just a training ground for future work for the Lord? Closing his eyes, Nick rubbed his forehead.

"Headaches?"

Nick nodded his head. He'd never had a concussion before and the doctor said his was a grade four, so he could expect symptoms to continue for a good month.

"That's to be expected." Dylan's voice was right beside him and Nick opened his eyes to look at him. "You sure you want to be here tonight? The day has been big enough for you."

The hall door opened, and Nick looked over to see Trent enter and make his way to Dave's office. A sense of calm settled over the frayed ends of his nerves. "Yeah. I'll be ok."

Dylan laid a hand on Nick's shoulder. "Well, let's get in there then. Dave ordered some pizzas to arrive in half hour."

A weak grin turned up the corners of Nick's mouth at Dylan's comment, as they made their way out of the hall and up the corridor towards Dave's office. Entering, Nick remembered the first time they'd all been called to his office before having the leadership team proposal delivered to them. He scratched the back of his neck and looked at Dave as the man perused his bookcase. This change couldn't have come at a worse time for Nick.

As if sensing his thoughts, Dave looked across the room at him. "Nick. Good to see you, son." Dave gestured to a chair. "Have a seat, take a load off."

Needing no encouragement, Nick perched on a stool at the desk just as Lexi appeared with a steaming mug which she placed on the desk in front of him.

Soft conversations began to fill the room as books were discussed, then chuckles turned to laughter as memories were shared. Nick sipped at the hot chocolate and watched his friends. Then Trent moved across the room and took a seat next to him. "How are you doing?"

Nick replaced the mug on the desk and clasped his hands. "I don't know."

The room quietened.

Nick felt his mouth press into a thin line as his teeth ground into one another. He looked at his hands; his knuckles were whitening. "Thank you all for being there for me today."

"I think we should pray." The reverent tone in Dave's voice felt like an umbrella of comfort and peace over Nick as he bowed his head and listened to his youth minister lift up a prayer for him and his work colleagues. One by one, his friends added their voices in prayer over him too. A dark weight within his mind felt like it was shifting as he listened to each voice, and when Trent finished the communal prayer, Nick opened his eyes – feeling a presence of power surrounding them. He looked at each of his friends, unable to express his gratitude, when Dave drew his attention.

"I think it's a good moment to pause and reflect." Dave placed his hand on Nick's shoulder and Nick lowered his head. Reflecting was all he had been doing of late. "Not one of us knows when our time is up. We need to listen for the voice of the Lord instructing us what to do with our lives, then pray for the courage to do it – even if it means going against what our own dreams and plans were."

Murmurs of Amen's answered Dave's quiet address, and while Nick agreed, he couldn't help but think Dave was directly addressing him.

The meeting with work that was scheduled for tomorrow played upon his mind. He was not feeling ready to answer the questions he knew they were going to ask about the ambush, or to identify faces in a lineup, or answer return-to-work questions.

Though, in the light of what Dave said, he couldn't deny the war within his mind to move towards something with more of an eternal meaning.

But was he ready to take over from Dave?

CHAPTER FORTY

Stomach rolling with waves to match a wild sea, Nick attempted his normal stride into the Richmond Police Station. His superiors had been very patient while he was in recovery, but it had been almost five weeks and now it was time to discuss his return-to-work program.

The moment he passed through the reception doors into the office, a round of applause broke out that sounded like the pounding of rain. Nick felt his face begin to burn. He gave a tentative smile to his work colleagues as he waved down their applause. He was hardly a hero. What had he done?

With great restraint, Nick tolerated the back-slapping and kudos given as he passed through the office towards Inspector Hartford's office, still unsure what the outcome of this meeting would be.

* * *

"How'd you go today?"

A bottle of sparkling grape juice appeared in his vision and Nick sniffed a humorless laugh as he looked up at Eddie, taking hold of the drink offering.

"I figured you'd need one of these." Eddie's voice held a note of sarcasm as he lowered himself into the outdoor lounge seat adjacent to Nick and took a swig of his beer.

Nick drew a long breath in through his nose and blew it out. The meeting had been intense. Going over details of the callout he and Geoff had responded too. Things he remembered. His recovery. The proposed return-to-work program. He didn't know if he could do it. "It was intense." Nick cracked the cap off the bottle Eddie had given him and chugged a few gulps, the sting of the fizz going down his throat a welcomed distraction from his troublesome thoughts.

"Hey, if it's one of those nights, I'll go grab a six-pack from the fridge."

Nick fired a mock glare at Eddie. He'd normally welcome the drinking jokes, but tonight he didn't have it in him. Bypassing the comment, Nick swirled the bottle in his hand. "I don't know if I can return to work, Ed. They wanted a date, and I… I couldn't give them one. I don't know why. They scheduled another interview in two weeks."

An awkward silence followed, and Nick looked from the bottle in his hand to his housemate.

"Knock, Knock."

Nick's heart spluttered hearing the cheerful voice calling and he turned, thinking Alice was about to walk through the door. He saw Hope step out of the house into the outdoor area to join them. "Hey guys."

Eddie was on his feet quicker than Nick had ever seen him move, hand extended towards her. Nick shook his head to remove the fanciful thoughts – as if Alice would ever be back. And even if she was, did he want to see her again? "Eddie this is Hope from church, Hope this is Eddie from work."

"Church eh?" Eddie clasped Hope's hand and held it a little longer than necessary. "I might have to start going again."

"Eddie." Nick groaned and drained his drink. He heard Hope cough a polite laugh and watched her avoid Eddie to sit beside Nick. "Yes, I think you should go to church again. It's very nice to meet you too, by the way."

Nick grinned at Hope's dismissal of his housemate. She turned to look at Nick. "Apinun."

There was something different about her – her skin had a glow about it. "Apin...what?"

Hope chuckled as she tucked a side of her hair behind an ear. "Apinun. It means good afternoon in Papua New Guinea."

A moment passed while Nick gathered his thoughts. She was so full of life, while he felt like a shell of his former self. His chest felt tight and he cleared his throat. "It's so good to see you."

Hope's smile softened. "And you too."

"Should I leave?"

Nick looked across at Eddie; he felt his expression was tight and tried to keep his voice light. "Well, if you feel that way, there's the door."

"It's fine." Hope laughed. "Just the last time I saw Nick was Christmas Eve. I go away on a mission trip and hear he could have died on New Year's Eve. So, you know, it's great to see him again."

The sarcasm dripping from Hope's words as she angled an even look at Eddie dulled the reality of her words, but didn't erase them.

He could have died.

He could have been like Geoff.

That funeral could have been for him.

Laughter broke into the dark spiral drawing him in, and he looked between Eddie and Hope. Eddie excused himself with a cheeky smirk, rose and moved from the outdoor deck back inside.

"What did I miss?" Nick's voice squeezed past the tightening of his throat the fizzy drink caused, desperate to pull himself out of the vortex. Hope gave a wave of her hand before her expression turned serious. "I heard you needed a kick up the butt, metaphorically speaking. How are you doing? Really?"

"Let me guess, you've been talking to Trent?"

Hope laughed as she glanced away. "Ah. No. But we should come back to that. Lexi told me everyone's very worried about you. By the look of you, I am too."

Nick pushed himself up and moved away. His heart was beginning to gallop, and his palms began to sweat. He didn't need reminding of how close to death he had come. How he felt paralyzed, not knowing what to do. Resign or push on? Resting his right palm on the verandah railing, Nick dropped his head.

God, what do I do?

"Hey."

Hope's voice was just above a whisper as Nick heard her come alongside him. He could feel her hand upon his back and her thumb's soft brush against the cotton shirt he wore. The tender gesture spoke volumes into the sense of hopelessness he was feeling, and he covered his eyes as he felt his face begin to contort with grief.

Gritting his teeth, Nick tried to restrain the waves of anguish physically racking his body. Memories began to flash through his mind of Geoff's funeral; the coffin moving past him, the brilliant sun that shone over the Australian and Police Force flags that draped the elegant cedar wood – it could have been him in there.

A sob burst forth from the hold Nick thought he had on himself, and he drew in a ragged breath. Hope's arms came around him. Releasing the grip he had over his eyes, he clung to his friend with his right arm as if she were a life raft in a turbulent sea. Her arms were strong and he could hear the calm assurances she spoke over the noise in his head.

Unsure how long had passed, Nick became aware that his breathing was slowing and his mind clearing, giving way to a feeling of embarrassment of what he'd let Hope see. He cleared his throat, not wanting to pull out of the embrace and look her in the eye but at the same time feeling it was time to let go. "Sorry about that."

Hope pulled back. "Look at me."

Pride thrown away, Nick rubbed the back of his hand over his eyes and met Hope's gaze, steeling himself for what she was going to say.

"I felt impressed to come by this afternoon and share something with you. Now, I think I understand why." Hope touched a finger to her lip in thought. Then looked back at him. "I'll be right back."

Nick watched as Hope trotted from the verandah and back into his house. Unsure what to expect, he began to chide himself for breaking down in front of her when he heard Hope's footsteps on the deck once again and looked up.

A large plastic looking container was in her outstretched hands, and he watched her with interest as she placed the container on the railing then looked up at him. "That's for you."

Nick raised the lid of the container and peered in. An iced cake looked back at him with the inscription: '1 Kings 19:5-6' written in icing across the top.

"Where'd you get this?"

"I made it."

Nick felt a smile tickle the corners of his mouth. "You made it?"

With an elaborate gesture towards the cake, Hope gave a nod of her head that sent her hair bouncing. "Yeah, I know."

"Why this story?"

"You know it?"

Nick gave a dip of his head. "Very well. I'm more surprised you know this story than the fact you baked."

"I heard it at the church I went to while I was away." Hope picked up the knife and sliced into the cake. "I love that God met Elijah right where he was and provided a cake for him to eat." Nick chuckled. Hope giggled before looking back at him. "I'm serious. Who couldn't use a cake when feeling down? But more importantly, God knows us so well and meets us where we are."

Lightness began to fill Nick's mind at her words. "I doubt the cake He provided Elijah was a double cream-filled sponge, though."

Nick watched Hope lift out a piece of cake and place it on a plate for him. He knew the story she referenced well, only, never had considered it from his own standpoint.

He was at his wits' end, like Elijah.

No idea what to do, like Elijah.

Nick took the plate she offered with an appreciation he couldn't express. Through his friend, he knew what the Lord was asking him to do at this point in time:

Rest.

CHAPTER FORTY-ONE

*N*ick awoke with an eerie awareness and lay still – staring up at his bedroom ceiling. His room was silent and, by the lack of light outside his window, it was still the middle of the night. Realizing he had dreamt that dream again, Nick rolled to his side wondering about the closing scenes.

It had been different this time.

He had broken rank and gone to the dying young man. He'd taken his hand and looked into those wild, unblinking eyes and comforted him – he'd spoken about Jesus.

The memory of the peace that crossed the young man's features flashed into his mind and he sat up.

A vague disquiet stirred within his mind. Was it significant that he was the only one that went to him? Why, of all the times he'd had this dream, had the ending changed now?

Nick wriggled the fingers on his right hand. He could still feel the claw-like fingers of the victim grasping his hand, until he had slipped away in death.

Restless, Nick headed to the kitchen for a drink. He had to try and think about something else, or he'd never get back to sleep.

* * * *

The day was warming up fast to its predicted 42 degrees, but Nick couldn't settle at home. He had to get out of the house. Since he'd woken up, the dream continued to play over and over in his mind. The way the dream ended this time – him sharing the gospel with the dying victim – was different from the way it had ended previously. And it bothered him.

He needed the beach. Had to get out of this stuffy neighborhood and get some space to think.

Grabbing his keys off the kitchen bench, Nick strode from the house with one destination in mind: The Valley main beach.

That same sensation of being at home washed over Nick as soon as he pulled his Clubsport up at the main beach carpark. The beach was empty, and it looked to him as if God had His arms open wide, inviting him to come and have some quiet time. An eagerness to be somewhere he felt close to God snuffed out every other thought in his mind and, taking his shoes off, Nick made his way down to where the water lapped gently upon the sand.

With the roar of the ocean in his ears and the tepid water caressing his bare feet, Nick looked out over the glistening azure horizon and let his innumerable thoughts run. The more the thoughts swirled, disappointment began to be the loudest noise in his head. Disappointment at his own despondency. He wanted to be a policeman but, if he was being honest with himself, he knew he couldn't go back. Perhaps that thug was right: he was weak. Lowering his eyes to watch the water splash over his feet, Nick pocketed his hands and scuffed up the sludgy sand. Sure, last year had been tough, but wasn't he strong enough to handle the job? Physically he nailed it, but it seemed his mind was letting him down. Ironically, he considered himself strong of mind, confident, intelligent, intuitive... his fists clenched. No, he wasn't weak. Fear had him in its grimy grasp.

Afraid?

Was he afraid?

Perfect love casts out all fear.

Nick let out a growl and ran both hands through his ruffled hair. "Love who, Lord?"

Some giggles sounded nearby. Looking over his shoulder, he caught sight of some young girls walking the beach not far from him. Their faces told him they'd caught his outburst. With a dismissive wave in their direction, Nick turned back to the surf before him. "God what is wrong with me?"

The sound of the ocean swallowed up the sound of his own voice. "I was sure my career as a police officer was blessed by you. Getting perfect grades at the Academy and blitzing the physical. Why am I faltering now? Is Dave right, you want me serving somewhere else?"

Memories of his meetings with his station about a return-to-work plan, and sessions with his peer support worker to process the trauma, played over in his mind. Everything sounded so straightforward but, as soon as he left their offices, his mind had clouded over again.

Frustrated, Nick dropped himself into the sand with a grunt. "Jesus, why do I miss home so much, too? I feel a part of me is missing when I'm not around here. Am I stretching myself too thin and that's why I feel everything is out of control, or are you trying to talk to me – through all this, somehow?"

The waves continued to roll in. The wind continued to swirl around him, sprinkling him with grains of sand. The sun rose higher and higher in the sky, beating down upon him like he'd just opened the oven when his mum was baking. No answers came in response to his questions to God. "Another day in confusion, Lord?" Nick sniffed at his own pitiful state and pushed himself up. "Well, I guess I shouldn't have been so hard on Hope when she couldn't figure things out. Is this why you're not answering me? Giving me a taste of what she was feeling? A little heavenly course on empathy?" Nick searched the sky from behind his sunglasses, waiting for God to answer him. Then, after a few more minutes of nothing but the roar of the ocean in his ears, Nick turned towards the carpark.

"Well, there's one thing I got clarity on while here and that's one thing I can put straight before I head back home. I'll go see Hope."

CHAPTER FORTY-TWO

M r. Meyer opened the door at Nick's knock and greeted Nick with a firm handshake and beaming smile. "It's good to see you, young man. How's that shoulder?"

Nick gave a tentative roll of his shoulder. The sling had only come off this week and he was still getting used to having use of his left arm again. "She's a bit steady on it, sir. But getting there."

"Very good to hear. Hey, come on in." Mr. Meyer swung open the door and waved Nick in. "Hope, you have a visitor."

Nick stepped into the cool of the Meyer family living room to see Hope swing her legs off the chair she was reclined on and face the entrance. She sat forward on her seat and clicked the TV off. "Hello there! What brings you by?"

"Sorry, love." Mr. Meyer interrupted, coming into Nick's view as he moved towards his daughter. "Why don't you and Nick head into the kitchen. Ryan will be home shortly with his mates, and they'll be after the TV to watch that dirt bike show."

Hope looked at the clock on the wall. "Sure, no problem." With a 'follow me' gesture, Hope headed off down the hall that led to the kitchen.

Hope was at the kitchen sink filling the kettle when Nick entered the room. There was a sweet bushy scent of eucalyptus that tickled his nose as he took a seat at the bench. Mrs. Meyer must be cleaning.

"Ok, so what brings you by on this blistering day." Hope rested a hip against the benchtop. "Must say, I'm surprised. Most people are hiding inside under the air conditioners."

Nick chuckled as he crossed his arms and leaned back against the backrest of the stool. "I've been down at the beach thinking and praying. I'm still no clearer about what to do, but one thing became clear and that's why I'm here…"

The kettle boiled and clicked off, drawing Nick's attention to where it sat on the bench. Steam rose from the spout in gentle wisps and curls and Nick felt his heart thump. The room began to draw out and he wiped his hands over his thighs. *God, chase the dark away!*

A cupboard door closed, and Nick dragged his eyes from the kettle to look at Hope. "I'm so sorry I haven't offered yet, but did you want a drink? I was going to make one." She frowned, her head tilted. Then her eyes widened in realization. "What triggered you just now?"

Nick lowered his gaze; his hands were a knotted ball. "The kettle." Nick heard his voice break and he closed his eyes, trying to remember the calm ocean and not the scene his mind was trying to recall again. "A kettle had boiled just before we were ambushed."

At the sound of a soft gasp, Nick looked up at Hope. Poised with two mugs in her hands, she had a look of deep compassion upon her face as she lowered the mugs to the bench. "Oh, Nick."

"You weren't to know. It's just something I need to work through." Nick took a long deep breath through his nose and let it out slowly through his mouth. "Yes to a drink. I'll have a coffee."

"Coffee, sure." Hope turned and moved towards the pantry then paused before opening the pantry door and turned back to him. "Actually, that's something I wanted to talk to you about. Coffee."

"What about it?"

"You know it's not good for you, right?"

The fog in his mind began to clear and he felt a chuckle try to work its way out as he looked back at Hope. "Says you. Miss Cappuccino herself."

With an accepting nod of her head, Hope moved back to the bench. "Yeah, ok. But not anymore. Haven't you noticed when we all go out, I'm either drinking water or herbal tea now?"

Intrigued, Nick raised an eyebrow. Now that she mentioned it, he had noticed. He just hadn't thought to bring it up with her. He watched as she pulled a tin canister out from the cupboard under the bench and then produce a small sieve-looking ball. "Anyway," Hope continued, "you definitely should quit the coffee. Caffeine puts your body in a state of stress and that won't be helping with your panic attacks."

A grin began to lift the corner of Nick's mouth as he watched her prepare what he guessed was a herbal tea. As Hope filled the tea infuser and dunk it into both mugs, an interesting smell began to work its way into his awareness. It was fresh and reminded him of flowers. He side-stepped her remarks about coffee. "What brew are you trying to give me here, Meyer?"

Hope placed a mug in front of him, then rounded the bench, her own mug cradled in her hands, and retook her seat next to him. "Just drink it. It's good for you. Leave your coffee-drinking in the year gone by – along with other things."

Nick took a sip of the pond-water-looking liquid in his mug and grimaced as he swallowed it. "What is this?" Nick coughed into his fist.

"Lemon balm. I got some for myself last year when things weren't going so well. I went to see a naturopath to help me get off the caffeine after learning how bad it is for you. She put me onto a range of herbals, but I think out of what I have here, lemon balm will do nicely for you."

Nick took another mouthful of what tasted like bitter flowers with an aftertaste of mint and swallowed it with effort. "What other things do you suggest I should be leaving behind as?"

"Oh," Hope replaced her mug on the counter. "These are just my thoughts. I'm not telling you what to do. But I think the police force should stay in last year. I don't think you're cut out for it."

With effort, Nick hid his reaction to her words and brought his mug to his mouth to give him more time to think about a response. Maybe he wasn't cut out for the police front lines, but that is where he wanted to be. It was what he wanted to do. He sipped the tea again – it was surprisingly refreshing.

"It's a nice tea, isn't it?"

Nick side-eyed Hope while taking another sip. He'd skip over what she'd said about her thoughts and move on to what he came to say. "Yeah, not bad. I want to tell you why I called in today." Nick replaced the mug on the counter and turned to her. "I've come to realize that I wasn't very supportive of you when you were, let's say, a bit lost. For that, I wanted to apologize."

There was the sound of a distant hum coming from the living room where Mrs. Meyer was now vacuuming, and car doors banging – followed by many young boys all speaking at once. Nick finished his tea and swallowed the dregs with effort. Hope smiled back at him before taking another sip of her tea. "Thank you, Nick. But you know, it was the kicks up the butt you gave me that pushed me in the direction I needed to go. So, don't be too hard on yourself."

The living room erupted with noise as a door banged open. Mrs. Meyer's raised voice could be heard asking for shoes to be removed.

"Guess Ry's home with his mates."

Hope gave a nod before finishing her cuppa. "Yep. Everyone retreats when those boys take over the living room."

"Speaking of retreating. I better start heading back." Nick stood and tucked the stool under the bench. "Ed's a bit like you Hope, hates cookin'."

Nick started back towards the hall while Hope tucked her stool under the bench and followed him. There was a cheeky grin on her face, and he knew his remark about her hating to cook was unable to be rebutted.

"I'll walk you out." Hope passed him and headed down the hallway.

Once outside, Hope pulled the house door shut behind them, silencing the noise the teenage boys were making. Nick watched as she hugged her arms to herself while she walked beside him back to his car. "There's something else you wanted to say before I headed off – isn't there?"

The blond bob around Hope's head began to bounce as she gave a nod before looking back at him. She looked unsure. "Well, fire away. You've already told me to ditch my career and coffee, I'm sure what else you have to say will fit just nicely with those two things."

Hope let out a soft laugh. "I just wanted to say, be careful out there, ok?"

An odd sensation flashed through his mind as he took in her earnest expression. His ordeal had affected not only him, but those closest to him as well. Understanding where she spoke from, he gave a dip of his head. "I will."

CHAPTER
FORTY – THREE

Nick sat atop his regular exercise bike, keeping a casual pace as he listened to the murmured conversations around him. Dylan was working the weights bench while Trent spotted, and the group of middle-aged men who had made Sunday night their workout night too, kept a quick pace on the treadmills.

Nick's gaze found Trent once again and he watched him with a critical eye. He'd not been able to bring himself to discuss with Trent what happened in the warehouse on New Year's and how the ambulance had known where he was. But it was gnawing at him. The counselors had picked up that he was holding something back, but how could he explain he believed an angel saved him? He raised an eyebrow at his own line of thought; they'd start assessing him for other things if he told them that.

Just then Dylan's phone rang, and Trent guided the weights back into the cradle so Dylan could answer it. Trent reached for their towels and handed one to Dylan, while looking at Nick. "How you going over there?"

Nick gave Trent a nod. "Feels good to be getting back into a routine again."

"Just take one day at a time." Trent headed towards his sports bag. "Pushing yourself at this stage in your recovery will only hinder your progress."

With an accepting dip of his head, Nick felt a smirk cross his features. It had been hard for him to rest. Every day waking up having an arm restricted and head injuries to recover from - not to mention the psychological trauma as well – had been hard.

And he was not good at sitting still.

The bike course ended just as Dylan tossed his phone back towards his bag. "I gotta head off. Mum needs a hand. She's still adjusting to Lachlan moving back to his apartment in the city." He rubbed the towel across the back of his neck. "You fellas going to stick around?"

Nick swung his legs off the bike. "Trent's right. It's great to be back, but I should call it a day."

Twenty minutes later Nick stepped out of the gym alongside Trent, fresh from the showers, into the muggy evening air.

Nick had found himself searching for an opportunity to voice the burning questions in his mind with Trent. But how could he ask those things? Just blurt it out or try to draw it out of him in conversation? Would Trent admit anything? Nick gave his head a shake.

"Headaches again?"

Nick stopped by his car and turned to Trent. "They come and go, but I'm ok at the moment. The counselor encouraged me to get back to the gym. Helps to work out the stress that's been accumulating within my body."

"It's good advice." Trent leaned back against his Ute.

Nick kept his gaze steady on Trent. His heart began to thump and he swallowed hard. "Listen. I wanted to thank you – for saving my life."

A nip of foolishness tickled his senses at making such a direct statement, but he had to know. He felt his breath coming faster as he waited for a response.

Trent placed a hand on Nick's shoulder. "The Lord saved you." Trent's voice was lowered and held a reverent tone.

"Yes. Through you." Nick pressed. "You were there. You stopped those men. You called the ambulance…"

A light wind blew through the car park and Nick felt a sprinkle of goosebumps run up his arms. "Was what Hope told me true?" Unsure what to expect now that he'd let his thoughts out, he watched as Trent gave a slight shake of his head.

"Nick," Trent's voice was low, earnest. "God wants to talk to you; He wants to lead you. He wants you to listen to Him. He has something he wants to instruct you in. Listen for His voice above the noise going on around you."

Captivated by what he sensed coming from Trent, Nick closed his eyes, resigned. His voice no more than a whisper, he responded. "What does He want me to do?"

"To be still and listen."

Be still. Nick had never been still; he'd always been focused and driven towards goals he wanted to achieve. Now it seemed those goals were taken from him and he had nothing else to do but wait for direction. He opened his eyes to see Trent withdraw his hand and turn towards his Ute.

Unsure what to say, though aware his question had not really been answered, Nick continued watching his friend. Just then, Trent looked back at Nick with a tender grin. "Like you've always said, Hope and her imagination." A soft chuckle emanated from Trent as he opened the Ute's door. "I'm flattered she thinks so highly of me. See you tomorrow."

Nick watched Trent back out of the parking space then chug from the gym's car park. The silence of the night began to ring in his ears as he continued to look in the direction he'd seen Trent drive off in.

Frustrated, Nick opened his car door and slipped into the deep, leather seats. He ran a finger over the steering wheel and let his thoughts run through what Trent had said, and not on how foolish he felt that he'd been drawn into Hope's parallel universe thinking.

Nick leaned his head back and took a deep breath of the fresh interior scent of his car. "God, what's next? Give me a glimpse of the plan if you won't reveal the whole thing. Some form of instruction. Where do you want me? What do I do now?"

Not wanting to go home, Nick tarried. The calm night around him drew him into a peaceful state where he was content to just be. He smirked. Not one thought remained in his mind and after so long of having a mind that never stopped, it was such a blessing to be still.

"Ok God. I'm still. And for once my mind is too." Nick's voice was just above a whisper as he spoke into the silence that started to ring in his ears. "Talk to me."

The silence lengthened. Nick closed his eyes in concentration, guarding the edges of his mind for any invading thoughts, and waited for what the Lord might say to him.

Time began to draw out like the evening tide and Nick closed his eyes and sighed.

It seemed he had to wait longer.

CHAPTER FORTY - FOUR

"Welcome back to the start of a new year, leaders!" Dave stood behind his desk; arms open as if to embrace the room with a broad smile upon his face. "It's been a roller-coaster start to the year, but we are here. So, let's get down to business. As you know, I will be heading off at the end of March…"

"Any idea what's happening to us after then?" Lexi jumped in, her expression reflecting the nervous tone in her voice. Dave gave a confident nod of his head and Nick narrowed his eyes on the man as Dave's gaze moved over to where he sat next to Dylan. "I do, Lexi. I believe God has chosen who will carry the team after I've stepped down."

"Who is it?" Lexi edged forwards on her seat.

Dave chuckled and he looked back to Lexi. Nick glanced at Dylan and found him watching the conversation between Lexi and Dave, but it was the look on Trent's face that held his attention. It was the look of someone watching something when they already knew the ending – a confident assurance but empathetic towards those who didn't understand.

"Nick?"

Nick tore his eyes from Trent to Dave. "Oh, I haven't decided yet..."

"Decided what?" Hope bounced on her seat before reaching for her bottle of water that was sitting on the coffee table. Nick gave a shake of his head as he read the room – he'd missed the conversation. "When I'll return to work, Hope." He covered, locking eyes with Dave. Lexi giggled. "Nick, that's not what Dave was asking."

"Well, I think it covers all bases at the moment."

Dylan gave Nick a few raps on his thigh as Lexi gave him an understanding smile. Dave cleared his throat and Nick looked back at him.

"I was asking if everyone is back on board for this Friday night? I've had a few enquiries from some new kids in town, so there could be some new faces amongst us and I want to get a feel for numbers."

Pushing past the elephant in the room, Nick gave a firm nod of his head. "Yep. I'll be there."

A sensation of concern settled over the room and Nick met each of his friends' eyes with a steadiness he was far from feeling. It had only been six weeks since his ordeal. His physical injuries had healed but the mental injuries were still fresh. He knew his friends were all wondering if he was ok to start another year of youth. What else would he do? In the confusion that his world had become, this place and mission was a constant; safe and consistent.

Just then Dave handed Lexi some papers to pass around the room. "Alright, let's continue. Nick, we are thrilled you're with us for another year. I think what I have planned for the kids for the first night might be good for you, too."

"Ooh, hearing God's voice. Interesting concept." Hope's cheerful voice rose above the noise in Nicks' head, as a piece of paper was placed on his lap and he examined it.

Nick felt an eyebrow rise as he looked at the title on the page. Timely, Dave. Very timely.

* * * *

"You sure you'll be right this Friday night?"

The night was muggy. Plovers and willy wagtails called into the still air from their treetop nests, while the song of crickets hummed a gentle note around the garden. Nick paused by his car and turned to Lexi. The light of the full moon above spilled over Dave's driveway, bathing everything in a soft blue, and revealed the concerned expressions on his friends' faces. "There's only one way to find out, isn't there?"

Lexi looked worried.

"What's on your mind, Lexi?"

Quickly brushing her hair out of her eyes, Lexi recrossed her arms. "I'm just concerned about you. I know what I went through is nothing compared to what you've been through…"

"Wait a moment," Nick pushed himself off his car.

Lexi held up a hand, her eyes closed. "No. Let me finish. We had very different experiences, but acute trauma reveals itself differently in everyone. I'm worried you're asking too much of yourself too soon, considering what you've seen and experienced."

Aware of Lexi's personal experience, Nick didn't want to disregard her thoughts. "But you were out and about within a week. You even did a university lecture not long after. What happened to me was six weeks ago. It's February already. I can't just stay home."

Her soft sigh was audible. "I know. Just, Hope told me what happened the other day..."

Nick looked over Lexi's head to where Hope was chatting with Linda, Dylan and Trent. He was filled with a disquiet that Hope had spoken out of turn, but then he felt Lexi's hand upon his arm. He looked back at her. Her eyes were pleading with him. "Nick, she's worried about you. Please don't be mad she spoke to me."

The look on Lexi's face, the gentle touch of her fingertips on his arm, and the hushed words she uttered, settled the flare of his nostrils and calmed his breath. Lexi took a step closer, "What happens if a broom gets dropped on the hall floor and the sharp crack of the handle causes a reaction in you like the kettle at Hopes? I mean..."

"Kettle?" Nick felt his mind clear, and he watched Lexi straighten as her fingers slipped from his arm. "She told you about the kettle?"

"Yes."

"That's all she's told you?"

A slight frown blinked across Lexi's forehead as a question flashed through her eyes. "Yeah... why? What else has happened?"

A strange sensation of knowing that Hope had kept his confidence filled his mind as he drew a long breath in. That moment he'd cracked in front of her, he couldn't have controlled. It had just hit him. Embarrassed as he was, Hope had handled it without a blink. He looked over at Lexi again.

Peace flowed into every inch of Nick's being and a tension slipped from his shoulders that he hadn't been aware of. He was going to be ok.

"Lexi," Nick looked back at his friend. Her worried eyes were focused hard on him, and his smiled softened seeing her concern. "Remember in the Bible where it says, 'for God has not given us

a spirit of fear, but of power and of love and of a sound mind'?"
Worry melted from her expression, leaving in its wake a peace he
was sure mirrored his own. "Yes. Yes." Lexi gave a soft exhale. "2
Timothy 1:7. That was the verse Dylan gave me before I had to
do that university presentation."

Remembering how much respect he had for Lexi giving that
talk at university in the wake of her trauma, and how she continued to grow in strength ever since, he gave a nod of his head. God
was so good, in all things.

"I will be just fine, Lexi. Not sure what I'm going to do just
yet, but I know I'll be ok."

CHAPTER FORTY-FIVE

"Nick," the inspector's voice was rich with warmth as he stood up behind his desk. "Great to see you. Have a seat."

The inspector's office was bright and airy with a new indoor plant sitting on the windowsill, Nick noticed as he closed the door behind him with a soft click. He would miss this place. The faces, the challenges, the comradery. But he also knew that it wasn't for him. Maybe it never had been? It just took a bit to uproot him from a lifelong ambition.

"Thank you, sir." Nick took the seat in front of the desk, then waited for the man to sit before leaping into the conversation he'd come to have.

A soft chuckle came from Inspector Hartford as he lowered himself into his high-backed leather chair. "Is this a social visit or do I need someone from H.R. here?"

With a wry nod of his head and lopsided grin, Nick handed the resignation letter he'd written out last night over the table. A flash of disappointment crossed the inspector's face as he reached out to take the envelope and place it inside the diary on his desk. "I am sorry to be receiving this. You have the makings of an exemplary Police Officer, Nick."

A wave of nostalgia washed over Nick and for a moment he felt himself falter on his decision. Should he take the resignation letter back? Flashbacks from when he was a kid pretending to be a cop, through to his graduation at the Academy, went through his mind. But soon the pleasant memories turned to crush him with regret once he thought about the night that started the downward curve of his career. He grimaced, remembering the things he'd seen that still haunted him in his dreams.

With a long inhale through his nose, Nick gave a nod to the complement his boss had given him. "Thank you Sir. This was a hard decision for me, but I feel it's for the best for me and my comrades. I'd be a liability if I stayed. Simple as that."

Inspector Hartford gave a long hum, as if he was considering what Nick had said, before leaning back in his chair. "How are the counseling sessions going? You getting out and about again?"

"They're going well. Working through things one at a time."

"Good to hear." Inspector Hartford cleared his throat. "Hey, not sure if the fellas informed you while you've been away, but we got to the bottom of the rumors that tried to draw you in."

Nick kept his expression cool and his eyes level as he watched the inspector, keen to hear how that one had played out.

"We had Intelligence work the emails back to a neighboring station, intended for an officer there with a very similar surname as you. After some questioning and sniffing around from Wayne and his team, they found this officer was the leak. From there, we found a few others who were connected to the cartel and locked them up too. The officers linked have been stood down and are facing a string of charges."

Just then the door opened and one of Nick's colleagues poked his head in. "Sir, the commissioner is here. Waiting for you in meeting room one."

Inspector Hartford rose from his chair and, with a nod towards his office door, began buttoning up his suit jacket. "Looks like we'll have to cut our meeting short, Nick."

Nick rose and offered his hand across the inspector's desk. "That's not a problem sir, I have another appointment I need to get to. Thank you for letting me know the leak has been found and the cartel has been dissolved. It's quite a weight off my shoulders. I'd also like to thank you for the time I've had working within this precinct."

Inspector Hartford grasped Nick's hand and gave it a firm shake. "It's been a pleasure. We will miss you around here. Good luck for your next step, son."

* * * *

"Did he say which officers were stood down?"

Eddie tapped his beer bottle against the mug in Nick's hand. Times like this Nick would have loved a strong coffee, but since hearing what Hope had to say about it, he found he couldn't drink it anymore. He grinned to himself, wondering what Hope would think if she knew he was on the herbal tea bandwagon now. "Nah, he didn't offer, and I didn't ask."

"Well, mate, that is huge news. You hear about these things but never expect to be embroiled in them. So, you're leaving the force? What will you do now?" Eddie sank into a chair and put his feet up on the coffee table.

Nick sat adjacent to Eddie, placing his mug on the coffee table to cool. "I've had an offer put to me, but I'm not convinced I'm the right fit for that job yet. Aside from that, I have no idea. But like I said to Inspector Hartford, I'd be a liability if I returned to the force."

"Liability is a bit harsh." Eddie took a swig of his beer.

Nick lazed back in the chair and crossed his arms. "I don't feel my mind is 100% on the job. Felt it getting worse since that accident Geoff and I first responded too. How do you go processing things you've seen?"

Eddie leaned forward and put his empty beer bottle on the coffee table, then rested his elbows on his knees. "I'm not sure. I do the required counseling afterwards and keep going. Maybe there was something about what you saw at that accident? What does the counselor say? Why is it staying with you?"

Nick leaned forward and picked up his mug. "That's what we're trying to figure out. I recall what I can of the accident, but I feel there's a piece missing."

"Like your brain's blocked it?"

"Exactly." Nick took a sip of the lemon balm tea he'd brewed. Not that he'd admit it, but the drink was refreshing and he did feel more relaxed afterwards. He grinned into the mug before taking another sip. Hope would never let him live it down if she knew. "I keep having dreams about it, so maybe one night the missing piece might make itself known."

Eddie chuckled as he rubbed a hand over his head. "Maybe ask that god of yours?"

Nick fired a smirk at his housemate. "Oh, I am. It's just not time to reveal it to me yet."

"Well, I gotta ask the hard question now…" Eddie's expression turned business-like and Nick raised an eyebrow as he replaced his mug on the coffee table. "Fire away."

"I'm guessing you won't be hanging around here now you're an unemployed bum?"

Spontaneous laughter burst out of Nick at Eddie's nonchalant tone that matched the look in his eyes. "Ah, mate. I was about to bring that up with you. I'll be off at the end of the month."

"Two weeks, eh?" Eddie held out his hand. "I can deal with that. It's been a pleasure living and working with you, mate."

Nick grasped his housemate's hand. "You too, Ed. You too."

CHAPTER FORTY - SIX

"Nick, Nick!" Hope called out, "bring them over here." Nick stood and looked over the stack of chairs he was pushing towards the stage, to where Hope was sharing a laugh with Lexi. "Aren't these going over here?"

A scratching, screeching sound curled Nick's toes and he peered over his shoulder to see Dylan dragging a table across the hall floor. "Stick to the plan girls. Nick. Over here, mate."

The hall door closed, sending a woody echo over their conversation. Nick lifted his hand in greeting to Dave and Trent as they moved across the hall towards him, then turned back to the debate between Lexi and Dylan. Their dispute over changing the layout of the obstacle course paused as Lexi approached Dylan, hands on hips and cheeky grin on her face. Dylan stood facing her, his hands in his pockets as if welcoming the challenge.

Bypassing the playful banter between the two lovebirds, Nick crossed the floor to where Hope now sat on one of the many beanbags that had been brought out from backstage. With an easy turn on his heel, Nick flopped down on another beanbag next to her and linked his hands behind his head. "Meyer."

"Call it. How will this end?"

"Dylan will cave in." Nick watched Lexi signal to Dave then point around the room, while Dylan laid an arm over Trent's shoulders and gave a slight shake of his head. Nick turned to Hope. Even though he knew nobody would be listening, he lowered his voice. "Hey, Hope." She turned to him, her jovial expression turning to concern as she looked back at him. "What's up?"

Awkward was an understatement about how he was feeling right now – vulnerability was new to him, and it still wasn't sitting right.

Last year he felt in control of any room he entered, any situation he found himself in and any conversation he was involved in. Now, something had shifted. He felt his grip on the Lord tighter than ever before, feeling that if he let go, the sinking sand of the unknown beneath him would swallow him up.

Nick cleared his throat. "I wanted to thank you for not saying anything to Lexi about that day you came over to my place. Lexi told me you've talked, and, just, thank you for not mentioning... that I lost it."

Laughter broke out and Nick felt his muscles tense as he looked over to the rest of the team. Lexi was giving Dylan a hug while Trent and Dave were realigning the tables. He turned back to Hope with a lopsided grin. "See. Dylan caved."

There was a distracting sort of smile on her face as she looked back at him and Nick withdrew his arms back from behind his head and crossed them.

"You know," the beanbag rustled as Hope leaned towards him, "I've never heard you struggle to get your words out before. Is it me or are thank-yous and sorrys new territory for you?"

Nick blinked.

He wasn't sure.

"Let's go, you guys." Dave called out with a clap of his hands that echoed around the hall. "The youth will be here in ten. Let's finish this obstacle course."

Saved from trying to figure out how to answer her question, Nick disengaged himself from his beanbag then turned to pick it up just as Hope did the same with hers. Together they maneuvered their beanbags to where Lexi was directing them. Then Nick heard Hope muffle a laugh.

"What?" Nick tried to see over the mound in his arms in order to place it in the right spot, when an unexpected bump on his side sent him off-course. He looked back at Hope and met her impish grin. "Oh, just remembering you having another humble moment there before. I think I'm enjoying this side of you."

On an impulse, Nick thrust his beanbag into Hope's. Hearing her footsteps shuffle back on the hardwood floor and giggle silenced, Nick readied himself for her to reciprocate. The shunt came and he chuckled just as Dave's voiced sounded from somewhere in the hall.

"Alright you two, can we finish setting up? I feel like I'm trying to herd cats tonight."

Nick dropped his bag to reorientate himself in the obstacle course they were constructing, a smile still upon his face.

It felt good to allow himself to muck around a little, to enjoy an unpretentious silly moment.

The night had a good feeling to it already.

"Why do I think there's going to be injuries tonight?" Nick dragged the beanbag into the place Lexi directed, then stood up to look over the course. Lexi puffed from her nose in ironic agreement. "There usually is when we don't listen to God. Right?"

"You can say that again." Nick offered his hand and Lexi high fived him. He remembered when he had received the impression that he had to break up with Alice. If he had just broken up with her in the first place, instead of back tracking and compromising on a long-distance relationship, he wouldn't have had the hurt of her cheating on him. God knew and was trying to save him from pain.

Nick inwardly thanked the Lord for the hard lessons he was learning as he looked over the course. It was impressive what they had constructed, and he had to admit he was looking forward to seeing how the youths navigated the course blind-folded.

Just then, the sound of cars signaled the night was about to begin.

"You ready for this?" The energy emanating from Lexi drew a laugh from Nick. Youth nights were like a charging cable for her, and she was on 100%. The new energy she had on Friday nights since being in the leadership role, never ceased to amaze him. He knew what the Bible said about doing all things through Christ, and it was evident in Lexi's life so, maybe he could do this role after all?

Nick gave an assured nod of his head. "Yeah. Yeah, I'm ready. Let's do this."

* * * *

Nick fell back against the couch cushions with a clap of his hands as laughter racked his body. He tried to regain his composure, but one cackle from the girls set him off again. The joyous sounds of their laughter reverberated around the hall as Dave re-entered from his office. He looked over to where they had regrouped.

"Are you all still laughing about Martin and Steve's run through the course?"

The girl's laughter pierced the air once again as Trent coughed into his fist and Dylan dropped his head into his hands, a muffled chortle following. Nick spread his hands as he petitioned Dave. It felt so good to be back without the shadow of his job lurking in the back of his mind. "Oh, come on Dave, don't pretend that as soon as you're in your car you won't burst out laughing yourself?"

"I'll be driving away praying that the message of listening to God's voice and following it to the letter will be what the young people took away." Dave resumed his walk to the exit, then turned back to them. "You right to lock up? I've gotta run."

Laughter died down under the clearing of throats and rustling of bodies off the couches. "No worries, Dave." Lexi called out, jumping down from the stage. "See you tomorrow."

"I'll get started on the kitchen." Hope called out as she jogged to the rear of the hall.

Trent headed to the wing of the stage. "I'll grab the brooms to sweep up, fellas can you start dismantling the obstacle course?"

"On it." In one smooth move, Dylan swung himself off the stage and began striding towards one of the stacks of chairs. "Let's go, Nick."

Working alongside Dylan, Nick moved the stacks of chairs back against the walls, folded the tables up and moved the basketball stands back to the wings. All the while he was fighting distracting thoughts in his mind about what Hope had said.

Had he been so haughty that he'd never uttered thanks and sorry before?

Aware of eyes upon him, Nick glanced towards Dylan and raised an eyebrow in question seeing him watching him. Dylan chuckled. "What's on your mind, brother?"

There was a faint knocking of the broom against the wooden skirting boards as Trent continued sweeping up in the hall. They couldn't stay backstage for too long. Nick lined up the last stack of chairs then turned to Dylan. "I haven't told you this, but Hope came over to see how I was doing the other week and brought me a cake she'd cooked…"

"She cooked?" Dylan's eyebrows shot up.

Nick nodded. "Yeah. It was a great cake. But that's not the point. The thing is, I broke down in front of her. No way I could have held it back. But she handled it like a pro…" Nick let out a breath as the memory came back to him. "Since then, I'm thinking all sorts of things. I can't make sense of it. I mean, I'm drinking herbal tea now, I'm full of apologies and thankyous…"

A slow grin was forming on Dylan's mouth as he spoke, and it was distracting and annoying. "Is this funny to you?" Nick glowered.

"A little." Dylan cleared his throat. "Do you remember your off-hand responses to me when I was struggling to express how I felt about Lexi? It's not easy to express your emotions sometimes, is it?"

Nick looked away. He remembered. "It seems the Lord is humbling me on all fronts of late."

A hand rested upon his shoulder and Nick looked into the empathetic face of his friend. That drowning feeling began lapping around his feet again and Nick clenched his teeth – he did not want to break down again. Dylan gave his shoulder a squeeze. "I understand, mate. You've been through a lot. You're seeing things differently. So, go talk to her and clear the air. I'll finish cleaning up with Lexi and Trent."

No sooner had he stepped out from backstage than Nick saw Hope trotting from the hall, waving a hand over her head.

"Gotta run, guys, see you all tomorrow. Happy Sabbath!"

Guess he'd have to chat to her later, then.

CHAPTER
FORTY - SEVEN

ick pulled up out the front of The Mariners Inn and took a moment to look over the grand looking seaside hotel. Its windows glowed with a gentle amber light, fairy lights twinkled over the upstairs balcony and muffled music from the live band could be heard coming from behind the closed doors.

While he was at church this morning, the invitation to watch the live band at The Mariners had sounded like a good idea. Though now, standing out the front, all Nick could think of is the noise that would be inside.

He still felt he needed quiet to heal.

With a heavy reluctancy, Nick pushed open the door and entered the building. A couple of songs, then he'd head off, at least he'd come. He'd kept his word.

As expected, the Inn was at capacity. The band was in full swing, with the dance floor alive before them. Lights were flashing over animated faces in different stages of conversations, while bartenders worked with single-minded focus.

Nick navigated the room and was about to head towards the dining area when Beth jumped into his line of sight. "Hey you!"

"Beth. What are you doing here?" Nick returned his younger sister's fierce hug, surprised to see her here during the school term. She pulled back but didn't release him. Her blue eyes appeared glassy as if she was holding back tears. "I'm so happy you're ok! Look at you, out and about. How's that shoulder?"

Aware she didn't answer the question, but feeling too emotional to wonder about it, he drew her in for another hug.

Lost in a reverie of how precious life was, Nick indulged the lingering hug when another pair of arms clamped around him. He felt his eyes spring open as Beth's bell-like laughter rang out beside him.

"Lauren!" Nick found a surprised laugh coughing out of him as he looked into the face of his older sister. "Tell me you're both not in town to see this band. They're not that good. What's going on?"

"Hey, man." Dylan's voice sounded behind him. "You made it!"

Nick turned suspicious eyes to his mate and, as he held out a hand, his eyes fell upon Lexi, Trent and Dave. Other faces he knew materialized in his periphery and he tore his eyes off Dylan to scan the room. Family and friends smiled back at him. He felt Dylan grasp his hand and heard his chuckle. He looked back at Dylan.

"No need to look like that, brother." Dylan stepped back and gestured to the room. "From us all, to you. Happy New Year."

Unsure what to make of the gesture, Nick looked over the smiling faces. A lump began to form in his throat, and he clenched his jaw as he gave a nod of his head. Not yet willing to trust his voice, Nick bought time by looking over to where the band were playing. His New Year couldn't have started any worse and here his friends were giving him a chance to begin again. His eyes began to feel hot, and he blinked rapidly before turning back to his mates. "Well let's get out there and start my New Year then!"

Raucous cheers answered Nick, and he felt himself lurch forward under a barrage of back slapping, while the room turned to white noise with everyone talking at once in competition with the band.

Five bucks says, I'll be here longer than a few songs.

* * * *

Nick stood at the base of the stairwell looking at the chain closing off access to the second floor. His head was pounding and he needed a quiet place to regroup. Ignoring the 'closed to public' sign on the chain link, Nick stepped over the barrier and made his way up the creaky stairwell into the quiet of the second floor.

The dim lighting soothed his tired eyes and frayed mind, while the music from the band downstairs was now muffled gave relief to his ears. With tired, heavy footfalls, Nick moved towards the balcony for fresh air. Could he leave his own party before the …

"Whatchya doing up here?"

Nick looked over his shoulder at the familiar voice and, leaning an arm back on the balcony railing, he turned to Hope. A startling heat licked up the back of his neck as he looked back at her. "Resting. Same question, back at you."

Hope sat at one of the tables just back from the balcony, phone illuminated next to her on the table. She ran a hand up the back of her hair as though she was thinking. "Ah, I know this sounds odd, but I kind of felt a bit out of place tonight. The music, the dancing… all things I used to live and breathe for felt a bit… empty."

Hope stood and made her way to the balcony. The moonlight illuminated her blond hair a silvery-blue. Nick took in her profile as her gaze was set over the ocean and waited for her to finish saying what was on her mind. She turned to him. "So, how are you handling tonight? Loads of people down there are trying to have a moment with you."

Nick chuckled at her change of topic and looked away. "Minus one. Ed's looking for you."

The laugh that came from Hope drew his attention back to her. A slow smile began to turn up the corners of his mouth, and he found himself laughing with her.

"Well, he won't find me up here."

Nick leaned over the balcony, resting his arms on the railing. "Correct. You're safe here. Ed follows the rules. He'd see the chain link across the stairs and wouldn't think to cross it."

Hope laughed again as she rested her arms over the railing too. Nick glanced at her.

"So, you never answered my question." Hope set her gaze upon him and Nick blew his breath out. How to answer that? He'd had such a great night, but it was too much too soon. In every conversation, he sensed what his loved ones really wanted to ask. The night felt forced with a pile of pretense on top of his freshly healed wounds. He was tired. "I'm ok."

Her gaze bore into his as she dropped her chin and raised an eyebrow.

He chuckled. "Really. It's been a great night. Who's behind it?"

"Lexi." Hope grinned as she looked back over the ocean. "She suggested the idea and we just ran with it. I don't think she knew it'd be this big, though." Hope looked back at him and sighed. "You've just got too many people out there that love you, I'm afraid."

Nick felt his throat thickening and he rubbed his forehead. Hope's comment had left him raw, reminding him that the aspects of his life he had thought so little of before, now held the deepest meaning to him.

"Nick? You, ok?"

Nick gave a nod of his head then, drawing a long breath in, he looked back at his friend. He could see the worry in her eyes. "Yeah. I will be."

The silence between them lengthened and he found himself admiring the growth he had seen in her recently. Her compassion, her new capacity to think of others...just then his mind wandered and without warning he found himself admiring her in other ways – the shape of her nose, her hair, the tilt of her chin... Surprised, he dropped his head and looked away with a breathy chuckle.

That was interesting. Nick raised his head and looked over the ocean, trying to move past the thought of kissing her that had speared into his mind. Yet, he wondered if he'd sensed the same coming from her.

"I'm flattered." Hope's voice was light. Was she laughing at him or flirting?

"For what?" Nick looked back at her, a grin playing upon his lips.

Hope tipped her chin, but then she folded her arms. "You're not the only one who can read someone, you know."

Nick resumed his lazing over the railing. "I didn't say anything."

Hope leant over the railing beside him. "You didn't have to." She sighed. "Look, Nick, you know I care for you – we all do. But you have to know that we're just friends."

Nick continued staring out over the ocean, avoiding her gaze. Where did that thought come from? Did he want more than friendship with Hope or was he just responding to her care when the chips were down?

Her hand rested upon his arm and Nick glanced at her. There was a sisterly warmth coming from her and he knew it was the latter.

"Can't say you've never thought about it, Meyer."

A chortle bubbled out of Hope as she thumped him on the arm. She never could be serious for too long – this was Hope, after all. "In your dreams, Marshall. In your dreams!"

Yeah, she had.

CHAPTER FORTY - EIGHT

*R*oused by the sound of Eddie's subwoofers pounding out a thumping beat, Nick peeled his eyes open and stared at his bedroom ceiling bathed in the morning sunlight.

It was moving day. Again.

He was not going to miss Eddie's taste in music.

Last night had been a big night, and he was exhausted. His head still throbbed faintly and his shoulder was aching. Thoughts of his conversation with Hope came back to mind and he smiled ruefully. Not only had he missed his opportunity to talk to her about Trent, but another issue between them had been dealt with. One he'd certainly not seen coming.

But he still had to talk to her about Trent.

Perhaps sometime today he could pull her aside and let her know he was starting to think Trent really wasn't what she was convinced of. Certainly, he'd allowed himself to get swept up with the idea that Trent was an angel, but the more he thought about it, his rational police officer brain was considering it to just be circumstantial. The man was always in prayer and he never missed an opportunity to open his Bible. Perhaps the Lord's voice was just clearer to him because of that?

With a prayer of thanks that his friends were coming around to help pack up his room and load the trailer, Nick rolled out of bed and made his way to the bathroom for a shower.

He needed help waking up – something that wasn't coffee.

That same dream had interrupted his sleep again. He felt so close to figuring out why his mind would not give up on it, and he knew the recent detail of his witnessing to the victim was the key to unlock the mystery.

So why couldn't he figure it out?

He needed to talk to Dave.

* * * *

The noonday sun was starting to beat down by the time Nick arrived at Dave's.

Sluggish all morning, he'd done everything he could to avoid having a coffee. Now, feeling washed out, he parked out the front of Dave's place and took a minute to close his eyes. They felt full of sand and desired to stay closed, but Nick knew if he stayed in his car too long, he would doze off to sleep.

Sounds of life greeted Nick as he approached the front door, and he pushed his sunglasses up on his head as he knocked. A vacuum cleaner stopped and, a moment later, the door cracked open to reveal Linda's smiling face. "Hey Nick. Come on in. Dave's in the Library."

The house had a fresh scent of lemon and some sort of herb Nick couldn't pinpoint as he moved towards the library. Whatever it was, it seemed to wake him up.

Dave looked up from his desk as Nick opened the door and peered in. "Got time for a quick chat?"

In a flash, Dave shut the book he was reading and moved it to the side of his desk. He stood and moved around his desk while gesturing towards the couch. "Of course. What's on your mind?"

Nick reclined next to his youth minister and rubbed his jaw. Where to start? "I've been having a reoccurring dream since that accident, but each time I dream it I'm remembering extra details. But... the last time I dreamt it, it had a different ending to the previous times... and I woke up wondering if God was trying to tell me something.

Dave's eyes narrowed. "What happened?"

Nick cleared his throat. "I dream the victim is calling out for help, but no one goes to him. Now, in the dream, I go to him and ask him if he knew Jesus. He shakes his head, grips my hand and I share Jesus with him. When he dies, I look up and there is a figure nearby who gives me a slow nod of its head then sort of disappears like smoke in a breeze."

"Ok, so how did you wake up feeling this time?"

Nick held Dave's stare for a moment. As he was describing the dream out loud it was like he was viewing it from a different perspective.

"I wake up feeling that what has been bothering me about what I saw that night, was not so much the physical injuries and deaths, but that I didn't know if the victims were saved. What if they weren't? Could I have spoken to them? To see people leave this world and not know Jesus – that frightens me to a depth I don't really want to consider, to be honest."

Dave pushed himself up from the couch with a grunt and moved around his desk. Nick could hear a drawer open and some papers being shuffled around. Dave moved back towards him. This time, he sat on the coffee table in front of Nick and handed him a card.

Unsure what lay ahead for him in the wake of his recent revelation, Nick took the card and looked at it. "What's this for?"

"I think you know."

Nick looked at the contact card for a training college in theology, then back to Dave. Something shifted within him. He did know. Dave was challenging him to admit aloud what he felt inside. He hesitated.

"Nick, listen." Dave's expression turned serious. "I've known you for a long time. Your walk with the Lord is deep. You take matters of the Lord seriously and you guard those truths with a steel-like resolve. You've always been sure your gift is service and, watching you grow in the Lord, I have to agree. You've always known yourself and had definite career plans. Now, I've not a doubt in my mind as to where the Lord is leading you. The question is, will you drop the plans you have for your life and follow Him?"

Somewhere beyond the library doors, Nick heard Linda's car start up and head off down the road. He lowered his head and rubbed his eyes. Him, enter ministry? "This is a huge calling, Dave."

"I'm relieved to hear you taking time to consider this. Ministry is not an easy area to work in."

Nick pushed himself up and pocketed the card. The future he'd seen so clear for himself was disappearing fast and a path he'd never have considered was now opening before him. It was like being a passenger and having no idea where the car was headed. That was not his comfort zone.

A feeling of light-headedness began to creep into his being. He held out his hand to Dave. "I better hit the road. Got a lot of thinking to do."

Dave grasped his hand in return. "It's ok to let go of the wheel and let God drive, Nick. See you Friday night."

With a nod, Nick made his way out of the library and towards his car. Interestingly, his thoughts were absorbed in Dave's parting comment. Was God trying to tell him something in that too? His stomach growled, reminding him that it was lunchtime, and Nick steered his car towards Main Street to grab something to eat before heading home to start packing up.

"Jesus..." Nick murmured. "Since I can remember, I've wanted to be a cop. Are you really wanting me to move into ministry now? I don't want to be a Gideon here and throw out a fleece, but I'm going to need some strong evidence that this is the way you want me to go."

CHAPTER FORTY - NINE

"And that's the last of it." Dylan's voice sounded from the living room of Nick's parents' home.

Nick looked over his old bedroom, filled once more with his things, then turned and made his way to the living room where his friends waited.

It was an odd feeling to be moving back home. Though he had not been gone long, he'd enjoyed both the freedoms and challenges of living away. Now, while his budget would get back on track soon as he reentered the workforce, he did wonder how he'd go under the same roof as his parents once again.

Finding his friends relaxing in the living room, Nick moved to the recliner and, flopping into it, looked up at the ceiling. He blew his breath out. "Thanks for helping me move, guys. I owe you all big."

A pillow clipped his chest and Nick looked over to the girls tucked up on the lounge adjacent to him. Lexi held a cushion on her lap while the one next to Hope was missing. Both were repressing their laughter. "It's going to be so great having you back in The Valley." Hope said, her voice edged with excitement while the others echoed the sentiment. Nick grinned as he took in Dylan and Trent looking like accomplices to a crime. He reached behind himself. "I'm feeling more like myself already. I missed this place – a lot." In a flash, Nick whipped the pillow out from behind himself and frisbeed it across the coffee table at Hope. She let out a yelp and dove out of its way, just as Lexi launched her pillow straight at him. Without a thought, Nick knocked it out of his way, just as he caught Dylan launching another one in his direction.

"Alright you lot, that's enough." Mrs. Marshall appeared from the kitchen just as Nick caught Dylan's pillow and lobbed it back at him. "Go outside if you've got energy to burn."

Laughing, Nick picked up a cushion and placed it back on the recliner before heading outside with his friends. He did want to throw out a fleece, but maybe cushions would have to do for today.

Either way, his friends were right, it was going to be great being back in The Valley.

* * * *

Nick sat looking out at the dusky view from his bedroom window, the card Dave had given him lay on the desk before him.

After his friends had headed home from supper together, he had retired for the evening to his room to think. A career in ministry? He wanted to laugh, brush it off and put on his uniform again. But he'd resigned as a police officer, because he knew it wasn't for him. No point trying to go back to it.

He knew God was calling him.

He couldn't ignore it.

Nick opened his laptop and punched in the web address to the theology university on the card Dave had given him.

Even while he scrolled the page and dropped a message on the 'contact us' tab, Nick still shook his head. He hadn't put the suggestion to his friends yet, choosing to try and work it out on his own, but if he was being considered to lead their group then the group needed to be in on it. Opening messenger, he dropped a message into their group chat.

'Hey guys, I'd like your thoughts on something. Until now, I've been trying to work it out on my own, but I need more advice and prayers. Dave has asked me to take over from him when he leaves. What are your thoughts? Nick.'

Nick leaned back in his desk chair; eyes focused hard on the message screen. One by one the bubbles of his friends' chat icons appeared until he could see all had viewed his message.

Dots appeared beside Trent's name moments before Hope's. A celebration emoji appeared beside Hope's name while the dots continued beside Trent's. Nick grinned while he waited to see what Trent would say.

Trent: 'In their hearts humans plan their course, but the Lord establishes their steps.' Proverbs 16.9. This is great news, Nick. The way you had chosen in life was not what God has planned for you. He let you walk your chosen path until it was time to remove you from it and put you on the path He willed for you. You have my unwavering support.'

A slight grin tugged at the corners of Nick's mouth as he considered the way God had uprooted him like a toddler who had wandered off and been plonked back in the middle of the mat where he should be.

Lexi: 'I couldn't think of a better successor. Look out youths! LOL! You got my vote.'

"Look out youths alright." Nicks voice came out in a slight chuckle. One thing he had enjoyed about the leadership team was brainstorming with each other to not only create memories for the young people, but to make Jesus real to them in all circumstances.

Dots beside Dylan's name appeared a moment before his response appeared on the screen.

Dylan: *'I'll back you 100% brother. When do you take over?'*

Nick sat up and positioned his fingers over the keyboard.

'Thanks guys. I have emailed the theology college that Dave suggested. Will let you know what happens when I know. I'm still adjusting to this blindside.'

Lexi: *'TBH Nick. I'm not surprised. Dylan and I have spoken about how you'd make a great replacement for Dave. What does Dave always say? If God brings you to it, He will bring you through it.'*

Hope: *'Amen guys. I'm excited! What happens in between Dave leaving and you stepping in as Leader, Nick? Do you have to do the course first?'*

Nick blew his breath out as he repositioned his fingers over the keyboard. *'My questions as well. Soon as I know what I'm doing, I'll let you all know – I haven't said yes to Dave yet, BTW. It's just, I feel that is the direction God wants me to go.'*

Trent: *'Follow the prompting of the Holy Spirit. He will never lead you astray.'*

Conversation speared off to other things and Nick sat back in his desk chair watching his friends interacting.

Was he ready to take this leap?

Nick rubbed his forehead. Exhausted in every way, Nick shut down his computer and crossed the room to his bed. His mind felt like the inner city at rush hour.

Muscles aching, Nick sat on the edge of his bed and began to massage his aching shoulder when his phone alerted him to an email. Yawning, he drew the phone to him and opened up his emails.

An email from the theology university sat in his inbox. He looked at the time on his phone. Office hours had long passed. He felt his eyes narrow as he clicked on the email – who was in the office at this hour?

He clicked on the email.

As his eyes followed the response to the questions he had asked, a feeling of excitement began to tickle the corners of his mind; a new picture began to take shape before his eyes. He drew in a long deep breath. Was he really considering this move?

Goosebumps spread up his arms.

His finger hovered over the 'enroll now' button.

He grinned.

Yes.

The traffic jam cleared in his mind and peace filled his spirit. He pressed the button just as a single thought swept through his mind like a sweet breeze on a warm evening.

"*Serve Me.*"

SHORT BIBLE
STUDY – NICK

1. Read 1 Kings 19:5-6. Why do you think the Lord impressed Hope to share this verse to encourage Nick with? How could it encourage you during low moments?

....

....

....

....

....

....

2. Josh's baptism raised a question within Nick about his personal life. Is there something within your personal life you feel God is asking you to address?

....

....

....

....

....

....

3. In Chapter Forty – Four Dave presents an icebreaker concept to the leadership team about hearing the voice of God. Can you hear the voice of God in your life? How can you make space for the voice of God to speak in the noise of life?

....

....

....

....

....

....

4. Nick was unmovable in what he believed, which caused clashes with his girlfriend at times. What does it say in 2 Corinthians 6:14-18? Are you unshakable in your walk with God?

....

....

....

....

....

....

5. In Nick's reoccurring dream, the victim is surrounded by people and yet no one goes to him. How can you see this reflected in the world we live in?

....

....

....

....

....

....

ACKNOWLEDGMENTS

The Victoria Police Film and Television Office for their time for answering my many questions over email and phone. It's incredible how much is needed to be known, to create a sprinkling of police dialogue throughout these pages.

My wonder readers, Karen R, Karen O, Suzie, Bill, Nina, Wayne for reading early drafts and being a fresh set of eyes over my work. I appreciate you more than words can express.

N.G.Wright (Editor) We have found each other by Gods good graces and while it has been a daunting experience for both of us to start working together at the fourth book in a series, I have enjoyed every correspondence and learnt so much from you already! Thankyou for your work in bringing Unshakable to life!

My Minister Pastor Marius, er I mean, regular Marius, and Youth Director Phil for direction on some dialogue and youth scenes. You gentlemen work in incredible areas for our Lord Jesus and are changing lives every day for the kingdom of God. May God continue to bless you both with good health and endless energy!

To all who have read my books, thank you! It is my prayer that you hear the Lord speaking to you through these pages and, if not already attending a youth group, that you may venture to a youth group near you. To feel the fellowship and joy from eternal brothers and sisters in Christ is unmatched by anything the world can offer.

"The Lord bless you and keep you; the Lord make
His face shine on you and be gracious to you;
the Lord turn His face toward you and give you peace."
Numbers 6:24 –26 (NIV)

www.ingramcontent.com/pod-product-compliance
Lightning Source LLC
Chambersburg PA
CBHW050426260626
47156CB00003B/1177